Daniel's expression hardened again

"You think their happiness doesn't matter to me?" he demanded.

"No, why should it?" Natalie said bleakly. "Tim's well-being came a poor second to your ambitions before he was born, and Ginny is the daughter of a man you apparently hated."

Daniel brought the flat of his hand down hard on the roof of the car. "Damn you! Whose fault is it that I'm a stranger to my son?"

When Natalie would have protested, he flung himself into the car. Looking at her with a face like granite, he said, "And to prove how much my son's well-being matters to me, I'll take you along, as well—if that's the only way I can have him. I'll even marry you," he said insultingly, and drove off.

Stephanie Wyatt began writing soon after the birth of her daughter, in the intervals snatched between straining fruit and changing diapers, and in the past twenty years has had a number of short stories and several novels published. She and her husband live at the edge of a small village overlooking the rolling Leicestershire countryside, their one daughter having flown the nest.

AN EARLY ENCHANTMENT

Stephanie Wyatt

Harlequin Books

TORONTO • NEW YORK • LONDON
AMSTERDAM • PARIS • SYDNEY • HAMBURG
STOCKHOLM • ATHENS • TOKYO • MILAN
MADRID • WARSAW • BUDAPEST • AUCKLAND

Original hardcover edition published in 1991
by Mills & Boon Limited

ISBN 0-373-17114-5

Harlequin Romance first edition July 1992

AN EARLY ENCHANTMENT

CHAPTER ONE

'AND to Thomas Albert Duke for twenty-five years of loyal service . . .'

Natalie tuned out the solicitor's voice as he began to read. She didn't expect her husband's will to hold any surprises, but Kitty had insisted on this formal reading. She looked down at her hands clasped against her black skirt. Kitty had insisted on that too, and because Natalie respected her sister-in-law's feelings she had gone along with it. But for Hector she had tied a bright emerald scarf jauntily at her neck.

'No playing the grieving widow, my girl!' he had commanded only days before he was released from his suffering, his voice still carrying some of his old authority. 'No one has less cause to grieve than you.'

Her grip had tightened on his wasted hand. His grey hair was trimmed as immaculately as ever, his sunken cheeks freshly shaved even though the effort had exhausted him. Her heart ached with compassion, and admiration too, for although he had sometimes succumbed to frustration he had never allowed himself to relapse into self-pity. 'Aren't I allowed a few tears at the loss of my best friend?' she said softly.

'A few, if you must.' His tired eyes smiled. 'But I'm serious, Natalie. I've already taken too much of your life as it is. Three years was all I expected,

5

and you've given me nine. So when you've got me
tucked up in the churchyard, you go on out there
and start living, you hear?'

Remembering, the faintest of smiles curved
Natalie's full mouth. What on earth did he expect
her to do? she wondered. Embark on a life of extravagance and dissipation? Start going to all-night
parties? She didn't see her future life being greatly
different from the last nine years, not when she
would have the sole responsibility for two children.

Oh, but he was going to leave a hole in her life!
She might not be able to mourn him as a wife was
expected to mourn her husband, but she was going
to miss him in a thousand ways, miss his lucid
common sense, his dry wit, the needle-sharp mind
that challenged her to use her own brains, even his
bursts of frustration at the limits his encroaching
illness imposed on him. Most of all she was going
to miss the affectionate friendship that had de-
veloped so surprisingly from their spring and
autumn marriage.

'That can't be right!' Her sister-in-law's shocked
exclamation made her look up with a start. Kitty
Gilmorton's intimidating manner had been per-
fected during her career as a top civil servant in
Whitehall and was enhanced by her snapping eyes
and commanding nose. All this was now directed
at the unfortunate solicitor. 'There has to be some
mistake, Mr Derry. My brother must have left his
wife better provided for than the paltry income
from a handful of shares.'

'I assure you, Miss Gilmorton, there's no
mistake.' The solicitor bridled. 'I questioned it too,

at the time the will was drawn up, but these arrangements were all Mrs Gilmorton would accept.'

'Natalie?'

'That's right,' Natalie told her astonished sister-in-law serenely. 'Hector and I worked it out together before we married. And *I* don't consider the income paltry. It'll be enough for me to live on very comfortably.'

'*Comfortably!* But...' It was a new experience to see Kitty Gilmorton bereft of speech. 'Why? I mean, Hector was a millionaire! What are people going to think when they hear he virtually cut you out of his will?'

'That I've got my just deserts, I should think, if you mean those same people who were so certain the only reason an eighteen-year-old girl would marry a man old enough to be her father had to be for what she could get out of him,' Natalie said with gently pointed irony, and watched her sister-in-law's colour heighten. There had been more than enough of those, nine years ago, and Kitty had been among them.

'It's a long time since I believed you'd married my brother for his money, Natalie, and you know it,' she said stiffly. 'You certainly didn't need to go to such ridiculous lengths to prove your point, and Hector must have been mad to have listened to you.'

'Why, thank you, Kitty.' Natalie was surprised into a genuinely sweet smile. Her sister-in-law's visitations during the nine years of her marriage had been a cross to bear, and, though Natalie had been grateful for her support during Hector's last few weeks, this was the first time Kitty had ever offered a comment that was even halfway complimentary. 'And you really don't have to be concerned,' she went on. 'Hector's left me ample for my needs, particularly as he made other provision for the children's education. Isn't that right, Mr Derry?'

The patiently waiting solicitor inclined his head. 'As Ginevra's and Timothy's guardian, Mrs Gilmorton has certain discretion over their income,' he agreed. 'Though Mr Gilmorton did make some more recent changes to safeguard the company and the children's inheritance. If I may proceed?'

Curious, Natalie listened with more attention, but the disposition of the number of shares to go to each of the children was much as Hector had led her to expect. And then she straightened in her chair as if someone had stuck a knife in her back, hanging on to every word the solicitor was saying.

'And who in the world is Daniel T. Morgan?' Kitty demanded after a stunned silence, repeating the name of the man whom they had just learned had inherited a block of shares which, together with his own holding and his control of the children's shares until they each reached the age of twenty-five, made him the new head of Gilmorton Industries.

Numb with shock, that was a question Natalie too wanted answered. They were both staring at the solicitor, but it was Duke, her late husband's seamed and gnome-like valet, who cleared his throat and said, 'I think I can throw some light on that, Miss Gilmorton.' He cleared his throat again. 'Mr Gilmorton was something of a philanthropist. Not that he liked it to be known,' he added hurriedly at Kitty's sceptical look. 'There's many a youngster with brains and potential and the capacity for hard work that he's helped to get a good start. Mr Morgan was one of them...'

Nausea stirred and began to seethe in Natalie's stomach.

'Started the New York branch of the business from scratch,' Duke went on, 'and within five years had expanded into two other American cities. Loyal as well as clever. Plenty of top American companies made him offers but he stayed with Gilmorton's. A bit of a prickly customer as I remember him on the one occasion I met him, and nobody's yes man, but Mr Hector trusted him.'

Natalie let out a long breath, almost light-headed with relief. If this Daniel Morgan was American, then it couldn't possibly be the same man. The Daniel she had known had been ambitious all right, she thought with a spurt of the old bitterness, but to become a barrister, not a businessman.

'Mr Gilmorton reckoned there was no better way of safeguarding the children's future than by leaving the company in his hands,' the valet finished.

Kitty made an only half-convinced 'Ummph!', but Natalie was almost laughing at herself for getting into such a panic. Just because the name was the same! It wasn't as if it was an uncommon name. And even the fact that the Daniel Morgan she had known had once had an offer of help from some industrialist who'd wanted him to switch to company law was just a coincidence. In any case, Daniel had turned the offer down in favour of his ambition to become a barrister. No, of course it wasn't the same man.

* * *

'It's come! It's come!'

The boiled egg Natalie was fishing out of the pan fell back in again and Kitty didn't even notice the water splattering all over the ceramic hob. Only Timothy didn't react, concentrating industriously on his cereal bowl until, toffee-coloured hair swirling, Ginevra burst into the kitchen waving a long white envelope. Then his spoon did pause as he asked, 'Well, aren't you going to open it?'

Ginevra's big blue eyes looked even larger than usual in her excitement, but there was apprehension lurking there too. With shaking hands she picked up a knife to open the letter then with a strangled exclamation thrust both at Natalie. 'I can't! You open it for me, Mummy. Please...'

Smiling sympathetically, Natalie slit open the envelope, then, at a quick nod from Ginevra, unfolded the single page headed by the name of the Oxford college, her smile widening to a grin that almost split her face as she read. 'It's all right, darling. They've accepted you.'

'I don't believe it!' Ginevra snatched the letter to read for herself. 'They have!' she whispered. And then, almost shrieking in jubilation, 'I'm in, Aunt Kitty. Oh, Mummy, I'm *in*!' She hugged her mother's diminutive figure then picked her off her feet and whirled her round the kitchen in an excess of excitement as she chanted, 'I'm in! I'm in!'

'Ginny, put me down!' Natalie laughingly protested. 'Anyway, didn't I always say there wouldn't be any doubt about it?'

'Not while you were cracking the whip, you didn't,' Ginny grinned, restoring her mother to her feet.

Breathless, Natalie said warmly, 'Oh, Ginny, I'm so *pleased*!' She knew just how much hard work it had been, appreciated too the competition there had been for places at the college. One arm still around Ginevra's waist, she held out the other to include her son. 'Isn't it wonderful, Tim? Ginny's won a place at Oxford University!'

'I don't suppose he has a clue what that means,' Ginevra dismissed with elder-sisterly superiority.

'I do so!' Timothy scooped up the last of his cereal and pushed back his chair. 'Daddy told me all about university, and how you need to go there to get a good start in life.'

How true! Natalie thought wryly. Not only get there but stay the course. She could only hope and pray Ginevra would make more intelligent use of her opportunities than she herself had done, and simultaneously there came an urgent need to warn her daughter to stick to her studies, put her on her guard against falling in love, help her build some kind of defence against the kind of mistake that had ruined her own life.

But, as she watched a little of Ginevra's glow dim at this reminder that her father was no longer around to see her triumph, she knew this wasn't the moment, so she said bracingly, 'Yes, it's a great pity he didn't live long enough to see you succeed, Ginny, but I know he would be proud of you. Very proud indeed.'

The young girl's vulnerable mouth trembled and she ducked her head in acknowledgement. 'Yes. And I know who's responsible for that,' she said softly. 'Before you came along I hardly knew him. It was *you* who made us into a family.'

Natalie was so touched that emotion closed her throat. How could she think in terms of her life being ruined when she had been given the priceless gift of her son and this daughter she couldn't have loved more if she had indeed given her birth?

Kitty Gilmorton's commanding nose might have been built for expressing disapproval of such sentimentality and her snort brought them down to earth. 'Presumably the place depends on your A Level results?' she reminded her euphoric niece.

Ginevra grimaced. 'Don't remind me!'

'Well, if you're going to get to school at all today, you have a bus to catch,' her aunt reminded her briskly, putting the rescued boiled egg in Ginevra's place.

'Oh, help!' The young girl grabbed a slice of now-cold toast. 'Actually, Eddie's Express is quite a lot of fun.'

Priorsford was a tiny village not on any bus route but Eddie Mothersole, landlord of the Green Boy, ran a minibus service to Honiton, taking the children to and from school and the housewives to do their shopping or link up with the buses to Exeter or Sidmouth.

Natalie turned to Timothy, who was swinging between the backs of two chairs. 'Hands and face, young man. And don't forget your plimsolls. Isn't it your sports today?'

'Even so, I hate it without a car,' Ginevra mumbled through a mouthful of boiled egg as her brother thundered upstairs. 'Just when I'd passed my test, too, and need to get in plenty of practice.'

Ginevra wasn't the only one to find it inconvenient, Natalie thought grimly, remembering her shock and anger when, only a couple of weeks after her husband's death, a driver had turned up without warning with instructions to collect the documentation and take the car back to London.

'It was a company car,' she reminded her daughter, 'so they were quite within their rights.'

'It wouldn't have hurt them to let you keep it,' Ginny pouted.

Certainly an international company worth millions would hardly have a pressing use for a four-year-old Volvo estate car, Natalie agreed, but didn't voice the thought in front of her sister-in-law, whom she knew was a shareholder. Kitty had never been shy of showing her disapproval of her brother's second marriage to a girl only ten years older than his daughter.

Indeed, Kitty caught her niece up sharply. 'I'll thank you not to pass remarks on matters you don't understand, miss. And aren't you going to brush your hair before you go to school?' She looked with disfavour on Ginevra's carefully disordered hairstyle, then, while the girl was still in earshot, 'That child needs a firmer hand than you're giving her, Natalie.'

Natalie stopped another outburst from Ginevra by a shake of her head, and when the girl had stamped sulkily up the stairs said quietly to her sister-in-law, 'At seventeen she's hardly a child, Kitty, and her father always encouraged her to form—and voice—her opinions.' She began to clear the table.

'Oh, let me do that. You go and get yourself ready.'

Natalie responded to the testy command with a gamine grin and did as she was bid. Her dress was already laid out on her bed: a crisp navy blue cotton shirtwaister piped in white, sufficiently sober for someone recently widowed yet cool enough for a late May day that promised to be hot. Pulling it over her head, she belted it around her narrow waist and began to apply a sun-block moisturiser to her fair skin.

She still got a strange kind of shock whenever she reminded herself that she was a widow. She didn't *feel* like one, but then she had never really felt like a wife, in spite of nine years of marriage.

Staring at that apparently cool and collected young woman in the mirror, she tried to remember what the volatile, passionate, eighteen-year-old Natalie had looked like. Not so very different, surely? Her cheeks had been plumper then. Maturity had added some interesting hollows, as it had been responsible for the disciplined control of her mouth and a certain guardedness about the dark blue eyes. Her hair was just as fair but no longer halfway down her back. Now it was cut into a choirboy cap identical to her son's, making them look ludicrously alike until you noticed the clear grey of his eyes and that appealing cleft in his chin, so like——

She slammed a brake on her thoughts. Didn't she have enough on her plate without harking back to past mistakes? And what on earth had made her think of *him* again?

She knew, of course.

A frown pleated her forehead beneath her fair fringe. It had been that name from the past turning up in her husband's will that was persistently reminding her of things best forgotten. She had expected that the man who had inherited the financial responsibility for her children would have been in contact with her by now, even if he did live in America, but it was three months since Hector's will had been read and she hadn't heard a word from him. That alone seemed odd, and then there had been the sudden repossession of her car. To add to her worries, Hector's estate was still not settled, and if it weren't for her job she would have been becoming actually hard-pressed financially.

Could this Daniel Morgan be the same man who had disillusioned her so badly all those years ago? It would be stretching coincidence a bit far, but it could explain why he hadn't contacted her. He would be too ashamed.

Or was she worrying unnecessarily? A complicated estate like Hector's would be bound to take time to settle, and the repossession of the car could have been the work of some paper-pusher in the transport department being over-zealous. Even the fact that the trustee of her children's fortunes hadn't been in touch with her yet had an obvious explanation. Whether he stayed in America or came to London, he was going to have his hands full finding himself responsible for the running of the entire company.

Brushing a shine into her cap of ash-blonde hair, she snatched up her bag and hurried downstairs.

It was no more than a hundred yards along the village street lined with pretty thatched-roofed, colour-washed cob cottages from the Lodge to the picturesque Green Boy beside the shallow ford over the stream that gave Priorsford its name. Timothy, his plimsolls tied together by their laces and slung around his neck, gave his mother a hug and ran off to join his friends, but his sister scuffed her sandals in the dust.

That something was exercising Ginevra's mind was apparent in the resentful glance she darted at Natalie before saying in a rush, 'Mummy, why do you put up with it, letting Aunt Kitty boss you around? She treats you like a half-witted child, and you let her! Why don't you just tell her to keep her long nose out of your business?'

'Because I would never be so rude.' As the gentle admonition only deepened her daughter's glower, Natalie explained patiently, 'It's only Kitty's way. I'm so much younger than she is that I expect she *does* see me as a child, if not half witted. And anyway, the habit of command is too deeply ingrained for her to change now.' Two years her brother's senior, Kitty Gilmorton had newly retired from a top position in a government department in Whitehall at the time of his surprising—many thought scandalous—marriage at fifty-eight to a girl not yet nineteen years old.

'Well, I don't like to see my mother made a cipher in her own home,' Ginevra objected with youthful dignity. 'I'll be jolly glad when she goes back where she belongs and leaves us alone.'

It was a sentiment Natalie whole-heartedly shared, yet fairness prompted her to point out, 'We were all of us glad of her help and support during your father's last illness, Ginny, and I'm sure Kitty herself will be thankful to get back to her own home. I know she misses London, but she has a strong sense of duty.'

Ginevra spluttered. 'You mean she's just plain bossy!'

Natalie grinned. 'Oh, well, it does me no harm to humour her, and as to her bossiness...' Her voice warmed still further to a throaty chuckle. 'I've found it simpler to let her have her say and just quietly get on with doing things *my* way. So much easier on everyone than direct confrontation, and much more effective.'

No one had been more surprised than Hector Gilmorton to discover in the young and apparently malleable girl he had married a core of steel, born of the long years of parental neglect, forged by the anguish of her betrayal and burnished by responsibilities many women ten years her senior would have quailed at, a strength of will all the more effective for being applied quietly and without fuss.

For the first time beginning to be able to recognise this for herself, Ginevra kissed her mother fiercely before hurrying off after her brother.

The Lodge stood just inside the gates of Priorscombe House, red brick because it had been a Victorian addition, embellished by carved bargeboards that gave it the look of a chalet, the modern extension built in the same style. Natalie wheeled her bicycle from the now-empty garage and began to pedal up the mile-long drive that wound beside a chattering stream along the bottom of the combe to the big house that had once been her home until her father had sold it to Gilmorton Industries to be turned into the company training centre.

Not that she regretted losing it. Priorscombe had never been a happy house, not even when her mother had been alive. Her father had been—still was, for that matter, living on the proceeds of the sale on the French Riviera—utterly egocentric, his selfishness frequently reducing her mother to tears.

The stone mansion at the head of the combe was no longer the 'Bleak House' of her childhood when she and her father had rattled around in it, seeing as little of each other as possible, sharing it only with an inadequate staff which was constantly changing because none of them could stand the isolation, or her father's uncertain temper. The rose garden at the front of the house, which her father had allowed to revert to the wild after her mother's death, was now a gravelled car park, and the stonework he had uncaringly watched deteriorate had, for the last nine years, been kept in meticulous repair.

Her job there had come about almost by accident. When her burgeoning pregnancy so soon after her much-talked-about marriage had excited the renewed interest of the gossip columnists, Hector had suggested they make the Lodge their permanent home. At first there had been a great deal to do, supervising the builders, redecorating and furnishing, and she had thrown herself headlong into the task in an attempt to block out her unhappiness. But once it was completed, and Ginevra settled at a local day school, the unaccustomed leisure had given her too much time to brood.

Again, it had been Hector's suggestion that she should go to see what changes had been made to her old home, and her own curiosity had done the rest. She had found the manager, Simon Chesney, in a panic, the secretary he had appointed not now being able to take up her job for another month, and the training centre due to open in less than a week. Although Natalie had had no secretarial experience, she had learned shorthand and typing in her last year at school and had immediately buckled down to help. And if Simon was at first dubious at having the wife of the company chairman working for him, his need and her willingness had soon stifled those doubts.

Of course she had stood down when his full-time secretary finally arrived, though it hadn't been long before he was diffidently asking for her help again when the girl left abruptly. This had happened a number of times over the next few years, Natalie taking baby Timothy along with her to fill in when the isolation became too much for the town-bred girls. And when Timothy had started school, it had been Simon who suggested that as she could accomplish more part-time than the other girls could full-time he should make her position permanent, an arrangement Hector applauded.

Dismounting to wheel her bicycle over the last cattle-grid, she looked curiously at the sleek black Jaguar coupé obstructing the front entrance, something strictly forbidden to staff and visitors alike. Circling it she made for the cycle shed then came round to the front to eye it once more before pushing open the massive, time- and weather-scarred door.

It opened straight into the great hall with its stone-flagged floor and vast stone fireplace, which was much as it had been when Priorscombe had been her home, as were the drawing-room and library, except that the easy chairs and sofas were smarter, the three rooms now used as comfortable lounges. The cavernous, old-fashioned kitchen, though, was changed out of all recognition, all streamlined stainless steel with every conceivable gadget to aid the culinary artist, while the formal dining-room where she had shared so many silent meals with her father now looked like any good-quality restaurant with half a dozen separate tables replacing the original long table, now removed to what had once been the music-room and used for conferences. The ballroom too on the first floor of the west wing had lost any lingering atmosphere of frivolity in its transformation into a lecture theatre complete with raked seating.

The various lectures and training programmes were all in full swing so there was no one about as Natalie crossed to an inner hall, passing through a door to a passage that led to the rear of the house, and pushed open the door of her office.

Before she had time to put her bag away in the drawer, Simon appeared at the communicating door. 'Natalie! Am I glad to see you!' he said, relief in his thin, harassed face.

'How flattering!' Natalie grinned. 'Or has some disaster befallen overnight?'

But Simon wasn't amused. Passing her a sheet of paper headed with the company's logo, he said, 'If this isn't a disaster, I don't know what is!'

Natalie scanned the memo then read it again with rising incredulity. 'They're closing us down? But—but they *can't*! Hector always said that a lot of valuable work was done here. It was his particular baby.'

'They can. They *are*,' Simon said flatly. 'I had it straight from the new boss man, Daniel T. Morgan himself.'

Remembering the strange Jaguar parked outside, Natalie's mouth went dry. 'You—you don't mean he's *here*?'

'Arrived before eight o'clock this morning.' Simon was prowling round her office, a tall, thin man in his late thirties though his gangling appearance gave him a more youthful look. 'Imagine a robot hewed from granite and you've got him. Tomorrow he's going to start interviewing the staff, sorting out those he can absorb elsewhere in the company and negotiating redundancy pay for the rest.' He sighed heavily. 'There are going to be a lot of people out of a job and with not much prospect of getting another around here.'

Including me, Natalie realised with the feeling of dropping in a fast lift. The delay in the settlement of her husband's estate hadn't mattered too much while she still had her job, but without it . . .

Her panicky uncertainty about her future and her sick apprehension at the immediate prospect of learning the identity of the man in whom her husband had placed such trust suddenly flared into righteous anger. 'For someone who owes his past success as well as his present position of power entirely to the help he received from my husband over the years, it does seem particularly mean-spirited to deny even the most basic help to others,' she said scathingly, not noticing Simon's desperate shushing motions until it was too late.

It was a high, wide doorway but the big man seemed to fill it. Natalie stared at him with a feeling of inevitability, her heart seeming to skip then picking up a thunderous beat that made a roaring in her ears.

'Daniel!' she whispered. Her gaze was met and held, and for long, breathless moments the last nine years might never have been, the deceit and betrayal and anguish forgotten.

Simon said in a chagrined voice, 'I suppose I should have realised you'd know him, Natalie,' and the light in Daniel's clear grey eyes was doused.

'Mrs Gilmorton and I are old . . . acquaintances,' he drawled, coming further into the room.

Natalie hadn't noticed the woman standing behind him until he moved, but she wasn't surprised to see her. Wherever Daniel had been in the old days, Ellen Scully hadn't been far away, possessive and hostile.

'An acquaintance that hardly qualifies her to make such a slanderous attack on your character, Daniel.' Ellen's dark eyes gleamed with all the old hostility and Natalie could feel her hackles rise. If anyone knew that her relationship with Daniel had been more than mere acquaintance, Ellen did, knew too that Natalie was justified in her low opinion of Daniel's character.

No need to wonder now to whom the elegant Jaguar parked by the door belonged. Whatever had motivated him to give up his ambition to become a barrister and to sink his prickly pride in accepting his benefactor's help, Daniel had done very well out of Gilmorton Industries.

'I can only speak as I find,' she said quietly, ignoring Ellen and directing her contempt at Daniel.

'And I can only act as I find,' Daniel rapped back, returning her contempt with interest, 'since, presumably to satisfy *your* demands, your husband brought this company to the brink of bankruptcy. And now, Chesney, if you've finished socialising with our late chairman's widow, we have work to do.' He passed her without another glance, sweeping Simon back into his office. Looking triumphant, Ellen followed them and closed the door.

CHAPTER TWO

BANKRUPTCY! Natalie stared blankly at the closed door. What did he mean, Hector had brought the company to the brink of bankruptcy? Was the company *really* in trouble? Hector had never for one moment intimated that anything could be wrong.

In fact he had done everything to make sure the business *didn't* suffer. Knowing it could promote a lack of confidence if his encroaching illness became generally known, he had transferred his centre of operations down to Priorscombe before the symptoms had become evident, his marriage to Natalie giving him the perfect excuse. An office at Priorscombe had been filled with the latest electronic equipment that meant he could keep in touch with all the branches as well as work with his secretary in London as easily as if she were in the next room. Even when his loss of mobility meant he could no longer get up to the big house, all they had had to do was transfer the computers to his room at the Lodge. Natalie had long been convinced that it was being able to continue working that had kept him going so much longer than the doctors had predicted. Certainly in the last few weeks of his life he had had to let things slip, but not so far as the brink of bankruptcy, surely?

And to satisfy *her* demands? What demands, for heaven's sake? The only demand she had made of

Hector was that she *shouldn't* benefit from his wealth by going through a form of marriage with him. The injustice of Daniel's accusation stung her, as did the way he had dismissed her. In front of Ellen Scully and her boss too!

As the extent of the snub penetrated, she burned with resentment. How *dared* Daniel Morgan treat her with such cavalier contempt? Just because she had spoken the truth.

And this was the man her husband had placed in a position of power. If only Hector had taken her into his confidence! She could have told him that while Daniel might be trustworthy enough as far as business was concerned it did not extend to his personal life. But she had never named the man who had made her pregnant and then deserted her, and, having no inkling of Hector's philanthropic activities, she had had no idea that Daniel Morgan was one of his protégés. Of all the devilish strokes of fate!

She frowned in puzzlement. It was a situation Daniel should have found embarrassing, so why was he so antagonistic? Unless he was using attack as the best form of defence? She'd heard it said that criminals rarely felt remorse, that they could always find justification for even the most barbaric behaviour. Daniel wasn't a criminal but his snide reference to her marriage and her supposed greed could have been an attempt at self-justification for the way he had deserted her, and his talk of threatening bankruptcy merely to frighten her.

Had he really changed so much or had she been too blindly infatuated to recognise his ruthlessly selfish streak? So many years stretched between then and now that it was almost like recalling someone else's past, yet just for a moment, like a dream half remembered, came the echo of that golden glow when she had thought she had found the other half of herself and would never be lonely again, the unshakeable conviction that in Daniel something called to her that answered all her needs.

For, if she was painfully honest, she couldn't deny that her first reaction on seeing him again had been a deep joy, which was why his indifference had hurt equally deeply.

How foolishly romantic! Common sense should have told her that she could expect nothing *but* indifference from the man who had deserted her when she needed him most, who hadn't even acknowledged that last letter...

That was what she must remember, she told herself severely, not liking the way her thoughts were running, that he was the kind of man who, under the spur of ambition, had deserted her, left her to cope as best she could with his unborn child. How ironic that now he had the responsibility of safeguarding that same child's future!

'Oh, Hector, why did you do it?' she mourned, burying her face in her hands, trying not to contemplate the minefield ahead of her. But the telephone rang, reminding her she still had work to do, and after she had dealt with the caller she began to open the mail, putting her best effort into submerging her painfully reawakened emotions in routine.

Perhaps because she was left alone all morning she largely succeeded, but rather than cross swords again with Daniel just yet she avoided the dining-room at lunchtime, collecting a cup of coffee from the kitchen and choosing to work straight through.

It was four-thirty, later than her usual time of finishing but she had wanted to clear her desk, when the communicating door opened suddenly.

'Well, well!' Daniel's voice seemed to shiver over the surface of her skin, making her nerves jump. 'What are you doing here? If you're still hanging around for your lover, I have to tell you Chesney's got far too much on his plate to be any use to you tonight, and will have until he leaves here—I'll see to that.'

Natalie gasped at his inference, humiliation scorching her cheeks. He looked big and powerful in his dark grey, beautifully cut suit, the collar of his white shirt still immaculate even after the long drive down to Devon followed by a day's work— unless he had changed, of course. It made her wonder uneasily how long he was staying. She wanted to tell him that after what he had done to her her personal life was no business of his, but by not denying his allegation she could be damaging Simon's future with the company.

'Simon and I have a working relationship, nothing more,' she ground out between clenched teeth.

For some reason that raised his eyebrows. 'Working? *You?*'

He sounded so sceptical that her colour flared again. 'I'm the secretary here, working mostly with Simon but with the lecturers too, if they need me.'

A smile began to curve his hard mouth, but it wasn't a pleasant smile. 'So Gilmorton *did* find you out. I often wondered. And he made you work for your keep. Good lord, that must have come as a shock to your system!'

Natalie stared at him, a frown puckering her brow beneath her blonde fringe. 'I haven't the faintest idea what you're talking about.'

His smile became even more unpleasant, derision mixed with contempt. 'That's quite an achievement, being able to turn on that innocent look after nine years in that old man's bed, and not only his, I'll warrant. It'd take more than an old man's fumblings to keep that hot little body of yours satisfied.'

Natalie flinched visibly from the savagery of his attack. 'You—you're disgusting! How *you* of all people...' She choked to a halt, a *frisson* of alarm shivering down her spine as he advanced on her, backing her against the desk. 'Daniel...no...'

Realising his intention, she tried to turn her head, but a hard hand under her chin held her immobile while his mouth descended on hers. It was a travesty of a kiss, without respect, without even liking, and while her mind screamed a silent protest her body refused to recognise the punishment, her mouth softening beneath the onslaught, her lips parting, her hands creeping involuntarily to his broad shoulders. And in response to her softening his body hardened, the hips pinning her against the desk, giving her incontrovertible evidence of his arousal.

Her blood was stirring hotly when suddenly he thrust away from her. 'Don't try to pretend you found *that* disgusting!' he said thickly.

Feeling bereft, she stared at him uncomprehendingly for several moments before shame at her behaviour brought a scalding flush to her whole body.

Something flared in Daniel's silver-grey eyes as he watched the colour mantle her cheeks, then it was doused. 'It was a good effort, but it isn't going to work, you know.'

Natalie was still too horrified at the way she had responded to him to take in what he was saying, until he went on, 'You might have been able to wrap that senile old man round your little finger, but I'm far from my dotage yet. Oh, I'll grant you it was clever, persuading your husband to leave his company in the hands of your former lover, but——'

'What?' Natalie was incoherent in her disbelief. *'I* persuaded... Surely you can't think I...? Of course I didn't persuade him to do—— How could I, when I didn't even know he knew you?'

His response was a slow handclap. 'Righteous indignation down to a T! But you forget, I have first-hand knowledge of what a mercenary little bitch you are. All that scheming for nothing! You really should have checked that I was still interested, Natalie, because, quite frankly, I wouldn't touch you with a barge-pole.'

The words hurt, even through her indignant bewilderment, and though she was reluctant to lower herself to his level by bringing up his own highly questionable behaviour nine years ago she couldn't let such an accusation go. 'You really think I'd go to all that trouble for *you*?' she said, her voice every bit as scathing as his. 'I only wish I *had* known what Hector was planning. Then, believe me, I *would* have used my powers of persuasion...to make him change his mind. I never did tell him the name of the man who deserted me when I was pregnant, you know.'

'*I* deserted *you*?' For a moment he looked so angry that she thought he was going to strike her, but he got himself in hand quickly and there was only cynical amusement in his face as he said, 'So that's the line you're taking. Yes, I'm sure you're sorry your little scheme didn't work, but nowhere near as sorry as you're going to be. You planned on having me *and* your rich old man's money. Well, thanks to you, I'm now in the position to make sure you get neither.'

He loomed over her, his size and stance as threatening as his words, and for the first time she felt a lick of fear. Daniel had proved nine years ago how unscrupulous he could be in looking after his own interests. He had climbed high since then, and she didn't doubt that, whatever his twisted motives, he was still unscrupulous enough to use the power Hector had given him in order to make life difficult for her and her family.

A feeling of helpless anger engulfed her. 'How my husband ever came to make the mistake of believing you were a man he could trust I'll never know,' she choked, and swung on her heel. Still seething, she collected her bicycle and pedalled off down the drive.

The nerve of the man, she fumed. How *dared* he threaten her when his own behaviour both now and in the past was utterly indefensible? She found herself thinking of that punishing kiss and her skin heated again as she remembered her response to it.

How could she have let him get to her like that? How could there still be such ... *feeling* for a man who had ditched her without compunction? And what exactly was he doing here at Priorscombe? On the face of it he was here to close down the training centre, but he was far too important a man in the company now to concern himself personally. All he had to do was give the orders.

She was still frowning over all these unanswered questions as she walked into the kitchen, where she was met by an air of expectancy, Kitty letting the kettle brim over as she filled it at the sink and Ginevra switching off her Walkman, even Timothy pausing from the model ship he was making.

'Well? Is it true?' Kitty demanded. 'Is the training centre really closing?'

Natalie dropped into a chair. 'Good grief! How on earth did the news get round so fast?'

'Everyone was talking about it at the Ladies' League meeting. Do you know, they've asked me to address the next meeting, talk to them about working in Whitehall?' Kitty was almost preening.

Natalie congratulated her, though with a sinking feeling as she wondered just how much longer her sister-in-law was intending to stay.

'It is true, then?'

'Oh, yes, it's true. The new boss is down here to break the news himself.' An accountant's job to work out the redundancies surely, not a lawyer's, certainly not the man holding the principal voting power in the company. So *why* had Daniel undertaken the job himself? The question nagged at her.

'Daniel Morgan's *here*!' Ginevra exclaimed with eager curiosity. She had not been present at the formal reading of her father's will but had been told about its provisions. 'What's he like, Mum?'

Natalie managed to dodge that awkward question as Timothy said hopefully, 'Will the house be empty? Will it fall into a ruin?' a ruin he could explore at will being an exciting prospect.

Watching her son's expressive face beneath his mop of fair hair, Natalie was shaken again by his likeness to Daniel. Subconsciously she had always known it was there in the clear grey eyes and the identical small cleft in his chin, but now she had to admit to a similarity of expression too, and little mannerisms, like the pugnacious thrust of that cleft chin when something didn't please him. She could only hope and pray that Daniel's stay at Priorscombe was going to be a short one, and that no one else noticed the likeness.

His sister rounded on him. 'Of course it won't fall into ruin, silly. I expect it'll be sold for a hotel or something. But why is he selling, Mum? Daddy always said the benefits of the training centre far outweighed the expense.'

Natalie hesitated, glancing at her sister-in-law. 'He—Mr Morgan—er—implied the company was in financial trouble,' she said, toning down the actual words Daniel had used, 'but I can't believe——'

'Sounds as if the man knows what he's doing' Kitty said surprisingly, and, at Natalie's incredulous expression, 'I'm a shareholder and I've watched the dividends drop year after year. Oh, my brother did his best to keep things going, but he was a sick man, remember. There's a lot of money tied up in the training centre that could be put to better use. Anyway,' she went on into the sudden silence, 'it's the best thing that could have happened to you, Natalie.'

Natalie, her mind still full of the shock of seeing Daniel again, could only stare at her sister-in-law. Dear heaven, she couldn't know he...

'No need to look at me as if I'm mad,' Kitty admonished. 'For the first time since you were eighteen, you've got the chance to be *young*! Oh, while Hector was alive, having a job at least kept you in touch with people your own age, but now... It's high time you thought about yourself for a change, my girl. There's a big world out there you've seen precious little of. Now you'll have the freedom to get out there and see it, *do* things. Catch up on some of the fun you've missed.' Kitty waved the tea-caddy as she got carried away by her own rhetoric.

Natalie was too relieved that Kitty hadn't after all been referring to Daniel to really take in her words, but Ginevra giggled. 'Aunt Kitty, are you giving Mummy *carte blanche* to kick over the traces?'

Kitty spooned the tea into the pot, conscious that she might have been a little too outspoken in front of her impressionable young niece. 'I'm merely trying to point out that Natalie is capable of holding down a far better job than that of part-time secretary at the training centre, and that now is the time for her to stand back and take stock of her future.'

Ginevra groaned in mock disappointment. 'You mean you're *not* telling her to go out and find herself a lover?'

'Don't be saucy, miss!' As Kitty Gilmorton drew herself up in frosty disapproval it was easy to glimpse the imposing martinet who had once ruled a Whitehall department so successfully. 'I wouldn't be so presumptuous as to try to give advice on anyone's personal life,' she claimed loftily. 'But Natalie's not likely to find either a lover or a husband in this little backwater with only a couple of children for company.'

'I'm *not* a child——' Ginevra began fiercely, and to avert a clash Natalie stepped in with the smoothness of long practice.

'As I'm not on the lookout for either a lover or another husband, there's not much point arguing about it. Oh, lovely, tea!' While they had been talking, the kettle had boiled. She began to set out the tray. 'Let's take it into the sitting-room, shall we?'

'Then you should be,' Kitty persisted, following Natalie out of the kitchen. 'It's not natural, the life you've been living. Even I, plain as a pikestaff, had more romance in my teens and twenties than you've had.'

Natalie sighed as she slumped wearily into one of the deep, chintz-covered chairs, wishing Kitty hadn't brought the subject up just when she was feeling so shaken at meeting again the only lover she had ever had. The reason for Daniel's presence at Priorscombe still worried her. In fact problems seemed to be rushing at her from all directions and she found she was missing Hector more acutely than she would have thought possible. For nine years he had given her his strength and his support, even to his own detriment. Theirs might have been a most unusual marriage but over the years friendship and a mutual reliance had forged a surprisingly strong bond.

Ginevra handed round the tea, her mind visibly boggling at the idea of romance in her Aunt Kitty's life. 'I suppose Mum's worried about the training centre closing because it's going to throw a lot of people around here out of work,' she said. 'At least you won't have to worry about that, Mummy. It's not as if you're dependent on your job for your living.'

But I am! Natalie wanted to shout. Not only for my living, but for your support at Oxford if Hector's estate isn't settled by the time you go. She felt a cowardly impulse to spread the burden of her mounting problems around her family, but common sense told her that worrying Ginevra at this stage in her exams was unfair and there was precious little Kitty could do. Anyway, she told herself, her difficulties were only temporary. The settlement couldn't possibly be held up long enough to affect Ginevra. Fixing a smile on her face, she quietly agreed.

Natalie didn't find it easy reporting for duty at Priorscombe the next morning. Daniel's car was still parked out in front but to her relief there was no sign of him, or Ellen either, as she made for the comparative safety of her office. Hardly giving her time to smooth the fair cap of hair the bicycle ride had ruffled, Simon burst in through the communicating door, more agitated than she had ever known him.

'Natalie, why didn't you *tell* me you knew Morgan? Letting me make a real fool of myself.' His strained expression and tired eyes spoke of hours that would have been better spent in sleep wasted in trying to recall just what he *had* said.

'Because I had no idea I *did* know him until I met him yesterday.' When this didn't seem to placate him she added drily, 'As for making a fool of yourself, forget it. You must have noticed that Mr Morgan was hardly thrilled to acknowledge our acquaintance, and certainly gave no indication of wishing to renew it.'

'Hmm.' Simon stopped his pacing and from his thoughtful expression was mentally reviewing the little scene he'd witnessed. 'Not exactly friendly, was he?' he conceded before glancing at her curiously. 'So how did you come to cross his path?'

'At university. For a very short time and so long ago it seems like another lifetime,' Natalie dismissed, then, to divert Simon from any further interest in her past, 'Hadn't we better get on with some work before our new master accuses us of skiving? Always supposing my continuing as your secretary meets with Mr Morgan's approval!'

Simon looked annoyed at that last observation. 'I am still the manager,' he said stiffly, 'and until we finally close the doors I'll manage as I see fit.' But the flickering of his eyes told Natalie he wasn't as confident as he sounded, and, having had a glimpse of the way Daniel operated, she could only sympathise.

With a sigh he perched on the corner of her desk. 'OK, let's make a start. The current intake are being allowed to finish their courses so we don't have to send everyone home forthwith, thank the lord. Next week we've got the technical reps' conference, and as many of them will already have made their travel arrangements—those in Australia...Africa...South America might even already be on their way home—Morgan is kindly allowing that to go ahead too, which means the computer course can run at the same time as it's only four days. But everything else has to be cancelled and the people booked on our courses transferred to...' He riffled among some papers in his hand. 'I've got the name and address of the place somewhere...'

'*Transferred?* You mean Gilmorton's staff will be offered alternative training courses?' Natalie's pencil had been flying over the paper but now her head came up abruptly.

'That's right.' Simon looked ruefully sympathetic. 'I'm afraid your sounding off about our dishonourable new leader was a bit premature. Apparently running our own training centre just isn't cost-effective.'

Natalie made no comment. So she had misjudged Daniel's motives in closing the training centre, but he had said plenty since that there was no way of misjudging.

'OK, I'll draft out a letter to send to everyone.' She made a note. 'What about the visiting lecturers we have booked? Are we offering a fee in compensation?'

'Oh, lord, I don't know!' Simon grimaced wearily. 'Something else I'll have to ask the hatchet man. Look, can I leave you to make a list of everything you can think of that needs to be done? Morgan's interviewing each of the staff in turn today, and he wants me sitting in. That's something else I'll have to leave to you: making a rota and getting each one there on time, kitchen staff, cleaners, maintenance, gardeners, as well as lecturers. I should think twenty minutes each, don't you?'

'I'll get on to that first, then,' Natalie said, realising what a delicate task she would have juggling all the interviewees so it wouldn't interfere with their work too much or keep them hanging around. She reached for the timetable. 'Where is he doing the interviews, and what time does he want to start?'

'In my office, at ten.' He stood up looking rueful. 'I did think of banishing him to the office your husband used to use, but it'll be easier for you if everyone waits in here and uses the connecting door. I'd better go and see everything's in order and rustle up some extra chairs.'

As soon as he'd gone Natalie loaded the personnel files into the computer and left it printing out while she studied the lecturers' timetable and began to make up the rota. Well before ten o'clock she had the curriculum vitae of the first six to be interviewed placed on Simon's desk in order of appointments.

The time flew as one by one the people she had worked with for the last nine years filed through her office, all of them arriving apprehensive and asking questions she was not able to answer, some leaving resigned, a few—the lucky ones the company could find a position for elsewhere—positively elated.

While she shared a fellow feeling for them all, by lunchtime she still hadn't completed the list

Simon had asked for of all the tasks to be done before the operation was wound up, so while everyone else made a beeline for the dining-room Natalie fetched a salad and a cup of coffee from the kitchen and consumed them at her desk. And, although she worked as she ate, she knew it was only an excuse. Normally she shared Simon's table in the dining-room but today Daniel would be with him, and she was unwilling to risk another public snub.

She had finished the list and was completing the draft of the letter to company employees telling them of the closure of the training centre and cancelling their bookings when the door between the two offices opened. She raised her head, expecting to see Simon, but it was Ellen Scully who stood there, her eyes going to the tray at Natalie's elbow.

'I suppose you're hoping to impress Daniel with this display of conscientiousness?' she said snidely.

Yesterday Natalie had been too shocked at seeing Daniel to notice much about Ellen but now she could hardly believe the changes. Gone was the overweight girl with the thatch of wild dark hair who disdained make-up and seemed to carry a permanent chip on her shoulder with everyone except Daniel. Now she was a good two stones lighter, the pearly grey dress she wore businesslike yet worn with an unstudied elegance, the thin fabric outlining the svelte figure. The dark hair had been cut superbly and was groomed to a burnished shine while discreet make-up enhanced the good bone-structure her loss of weight had revealed. She looked what she was: a highly intelligent, sophisticated woman effortlessly holding down a responsible job, and she made Natalie feel like a country cousin in her Laura Ashley print dress.

She treated the snide remark with the contempt it deserved, asking coolly, 'Was there something you wanted?'

'The personnel files,' Ellen snapped. 'Daniel wants to study them before the next appointment.'

Natalie swung her chair away from the computer keyboard to pick up the pile of coloured folders she had ready. Ellen, reaching to take them from her, said, 'I must say both Daniel and I were surprised to find you *working* here.'

But Natalie hardly heard her. She was staring at the rings on the third finger of Ellen's left hand: a diamond cluster engagement ring and a platinum wedding band.

She managed to wait until the door closed behind the other woman before she slumped in her chair. Why feel so shocked? she jeered at herself. Hadn't Daniel walked out on her nine years ago to move in with Ellen? In spite of the fact that he'd always sworn they were only friends. Working together too would only give them an added closeness, so what was more natural than that they should make it legal and marry? Her hands curled into fists, the nails biting into her palms. She *wouldn't* let it hurt...

The same hectic pace was kept up all afternoon, and apart from hearing the deep murmur of Daniel's voice from the next office she was able to keep out of his way. But by the following morning there were only four remaining members of staff to be interviewed, including Simon and Natalie herself.

Rising to her feet as their top marketing expert left looking pleased with himself, apprehension churned in her stomach, but, telling herself this was purely business, she walked through the communicating door.

He sat at Simon's desk with Ellen beside him, heads close together, while Simon, in a chair to one side, was leaning forward to listen to their discussion. All three heads lifted at her quiet, 'Did you want to see me now, Mr Morgan?'

Daniel leaned back in his chair, one eyebrow rising sardonically as his eyes swept over her. 'Now, why should I need to see you, Mrs Gilmorton?'

The question was unexpected and threw her even more off balance. 'Because...I mean, you're seeing all the staff...about redundancy payment...' she stumbled.

He had always been a big man but he had filled out in nine years. Or was it the dark grey business suit fitting immaculately across the broad shoulders that made him seem so intimidating now? When she had known him he had always worn jeans.

'Redundancy?' he said softly. 'But surely you know casual workers are not eligible?'

Natalie felt as if she had been punched in the solar plexus. 'Casual!' she gasped, involuntarily glancing at Simon for support.

She saw his Adam's apple jerk as he swallowed. 'Well, Natalie *was* casual at first, just helping out between secretaries.' He gulped again, and she knew with a dreadful sinking feeling that he was torn between giving her the support his sense of fair play demanded and his fear of jeopardising his own future with the company. 'But I have to put it on record that she has always accomplished more in

the hours she worked than any of our full-time secretaries,' he finished in a rush.

Daniel merely looked sceptical. 'But her attend-
ance record speaks for itself.' He flicked over the
pages in her file. 'A few months ago, for example.
Days off...coming in and leaving at all hours...'

'But that was because my husband was ill,'
Natalie protested desperately. 'And I got all the
necessary work done.'

Something flared in his eyes but was gone before
she could identify it, the strong planes of his face
hardening still further as he said implacably, 'Exactly. Casual work as and when it suited you.'

Natalie closed her eyes despairingly, knowing it
was no good continuing to argue. Daniel was no
longer the student she had known, ambitious but
with a capacity for compassion. He was a hard-
faced businessman with cold, calculating eyes and
a computer for a heart. Why should he be concerned with her problems? He hadn't even asked
after the son she had borne him. He was a stranger,
a man she couldn't even like.

CHAPTER THREE

STANDING straight and slender in front of the desk, because at no point during the interview had Daniel asked her to sit down, Natalie asked with a quiet dignity, 'Then if I don't qualify for severance pay perhaps you'll be good enough to tell me how much longer I shall have a job at all?'

'Oh, for heaven's sake!' Daniel exploded with impatience. 'However gallantly Mr Chesney exaggerates your virtues, we all know you're only playing at working, so you might as well finish right now.'

Natalie flinched while Simon, opening his mouth to protest, subsided again looking dismayed.

She had been sacked on the spot! For just a few seconds she thought of the mountain of work to be done to wind up the training centre operation, and then she thought fatalistically, what the hell! Let Daniel and his wife do it themselves. Her wages for another week or so wouldn't really make much difference, and at least it meant she would be free to start job-hunting right away.

'As you please,' she said distantly, and walked steadily back to her own office, closing the door behind her. Crossing the room to her desk, she stared at the file she had been working on still displayed on the computer screen. Through the wall, she could hear the murmur of Ellen's voice and

43

Daniel's sharp response, and her hand reached out to close the program down.

How could a man have changed so much in nine years? she wondered numbly, remembering the handsome, rather serious and very protective student she had fallen in love with...

She had just started her third term at university. Her father was supposed to supplement her grant and selfishly didn't, so in order to live Natalie had found a weekend job as a barmaid in a nightclub in the city, reasonably well-paid but very long hours. The first two terms she'd had the company of a fellow student for the long walk back to the hostel, but this term she had to face the deserted streets alone. Not quite deserted, she quickly realised, hearing her own footsteps echoed by others some way behind. She quickened her steps, too frightened to look back, arriving at the hostel gasping for breath, but safe.

Maybe it was just someone innocently returning home like herself, she thought, but the following night it happened again, and although the pursuing footsteps rang against the pavement with no attempt at concealment she felt she was being stalked. And this time when she reached the safety of the hostel doorway she turned, staring at the figure who had passed at the corner. It was raining and he was too far away to see clearly but he was big, his shrouding anorak making him look even more bulky and menacing. And he was watching her. He knew where she lived!

Natalie determined there and then that she would take a taxi in future, even though it would blast a hole in her budget, but then she had a whole week to decide she was over-reacting. A decision that seemed justified when to her relief there was no echo to her own quick steps. It was pure nervousness that made her glance over her shoulder, and to her horror she saw him, no anorak tonight but still big and menacing in sweatshirt, jeans and trainers. Panic gripped her and she began to run.

It happened so swiftly that she was never able to put it together in sequence, but she ran full tilt into someone who stepped out of a dark gap between two buildings, grabbing her roughly, hurting her as he tried to drag her back into the alleyway. Her scream drowned out the slap of feet pounding along the pavement, but the next moment her assailant had let her go, fighting for his own life against the strangling arm which her rescuer had around his neck. Trembling, she watched as the big man shook him like a dog shook a weasel, throwing him to one side as Natalie sank weakly to her knees.

'Are you all right?' His deep voice was anxious, his strong hands as he lifted her surprisingly gentle. But for Natalie his transition from menacing threat to caring saviour was too much. She choked, tears welling in her sapphire-blue eyes, and the next moment she was cradled in his arms sobbing out her shock and fear against his broad chest.

'It's all right,' he murmured, rubbing his cheek against her hair. 'He didn't have time to hurt you. That's why I've been following you from the club, to make sure you got home safely.'

She lifted her tear-stained face to stare at him. 'I thought . . .'

His mouth twisted wryly. 'I realised when you started to run that you were suspecting *me* of having evil designs.'

Seen close to there was no vestige of the menace she had felt from a distance. He was older than she was, she guessed, the strong planes of his face those of a man, not a boy, saved from severity by a rather endearing cleft in his chin. His deep-set eyes were a very clear grey, looking at her with real concern.

She frowned in puzzlement, trying to make sense of what he'd said. 'I don't understand. I mean how do you *know* where I work? That I have to walk home alone?'

He smiled and she found her gaze drawn to his mouth, fascinated by the shape of it. 'I work at the club too,' he said. 'The official title is security, but actually I'm a bouncer.'

Natalie's eyes widened. 'At Spikey's? Good heavens! I don't recall seeing you there,' she added apologetically.

'Hardly surprising.' He looked down deprecatingly at his shabby jeans. 'They disguise me in a dinner-jacket and black tie. Anyway, your job doesn't give you much time for gazing around, does it?'

Her terror of a few minutes before was receding and she managed a laugh. 'How true!' Between filling the orders for the waiters, serving customers at the bar, dealing with change and dodging the wandering hands of the bar manager, she and the other two barmaids were on the go the whole night.

'I noticed you,' he said softly, and heat crawled over her skin. 'When I realised you were walking home alone,' he went on, 'I wanted to ask if you'd let me take you, but I was afraid you'd be suspicious of me and refuse. So I just kept you in sight till you got to the hostel safely.'

'Thank heavens you did!' The reminder of her nasty experience wiped the smile from her face and made her shiver.

He felt the tremor and, tucking her arm supportively in his, began walking her at a smart pace. 'If only I'd had the courage to *ask* you to let me see you home...' he said self-condemningly, and Natalie looked up at him in amazement.

How could a man like this need courage to talk to *her*? Men did sometimes pass comments on her hair, a natural ash-blonde and halfway down her back now because she couldn't afford to have it cut, but as for her looks... small and skinny, her face all eyes and mouth. He, now, he was... magnificent was the only word to describe him. Not strictly handsome, perhaps, but certainly good-looking enough not to have suffered from female brush-offs. She was very much aware of his hard muscles as his arm held hers.

He took her right to the door of the hostel. She looked up at him, the memory of her fright turning the deep blue of her eyes to violet. 'I don't know how to thank you,' she said. 'If you hadn't——'

His clasp on her hand was warm. 'Don't let it prey on your mind. Believe me, you were never in any real danger for a moment.'

She *did* believe him. He had a kind of presence that encouraged trust and confidence. And that was odd, because she didn't know him from Adam. 'I— I don't even know your name,' she stammered.

'Daniel. Daniel Morgan.' Again the rather serious lines of his face lightened miraculously as he smiled. 'And, in case you're wondering, I'm not planning on making a career in nightclubs, just keeping the wolf from the door until I've taken my finals. Like you, I'm a student. Studying law.'

Natalie responded to his smile as a flower responded to the sun. 'Natalie Quinn, and I'm coming to the end of my first year doing business studies.'

'Natalie...' He repeated her name slowly, as if savouring it. 'It suits you. Sort of dainty and feminine.'

Her heartbeat quickened. 'Daniel suits you too,' she said shyly. 'Strong and brave, like Daniel who dared the lions' den.'

She had disconcerted him, embarrassment sitting oddly on that strong, determined face. 'Nothing brave about chasing off that cowardly creep,' he said gruffly, then, as Natalie winced at the memory, 'Sorry, I didn't mean to remind you.' He frowned. 'I don't suppose there's such a thing as a drop of whisky in this hen-house?' And when she shook her head, 'It'll have to be cocoa, then. Help you to sleep.' He waited until she had unlocked the door then added softly, 'Goodnight, Natalie. I'll see you tomorrow.'

After that Natalie never had to walk home from her job alone again. They became the high spot of her week, the early hours of Saturday and Sunday mornings, and she often found herself thinking about the attractive but rather reserved law student when she should have been paying attention to lectures. She learned he was an orphan, brought up in a children's home from the age of eleven, that well-meaning people had discouraged him from taking up law as it was a career that needed a private income, or at least family backing, to get established. He told her about the labouring jobs he had taken on, hard and often dangerous but well paid, living frugally in order to save most of what he earned, how he had finally got his wish and now, at the age of twenty-four, was about to take his finals for his law degree, the first step towards his long-held ambition of becoming a barrister.

'At the beginning of this term I did have my hopes raised about my way being made a bit smoother,' he said, and there was a cynical curl to his mouth. 'Some wealthy businessman buying his ticket to heaven, helping the deserving poor. Trouble was, I didn't like the strings attached to his offer. He wasn't interested in helping me to become a barrister, only in turning me into some kind of business executive whizz kid. So I had to tell Mr Moneybags what he could do with his offer.'

Compared with the obstacles Daniel had overcome, Natalie's own difficulties seemed trivial and her admiration for his tenacity and self-discipline was transparent, as was the fact that she found him devastatingly attractive. Even so, it was two weeks before he kissed her at the door of the hostel.

'You'll wait for me to collect you next Friday night?' he asked gruffly.

She nodded, thinking of the week that must pass until then, expecting him to turn away with his usual brisk goodbye. But he stayed there, staring down into her uplifted face, his skin drained of colour by the orange street-lamps, his grey eyes shadowed, then his head lowered and his mouth touched hers in a kiss that was tentative at first, as if he doubted the wisdom of giving in to temptation. But as Natalie's lips moved beneath his in shy response it was as if she had detonated an explosive charge. His hands which had been gently fondling her slender shoulders, slid round her back, gathering her to him so fiercely that he lifted her off her feet, his kiss deepening to that of a thirsty man unexpectedly finding water in the desert. Both of them were trembling when they finally drew apart, and Natalie went to bed that night with her heart singing.

But it was two more weeks before Daniel suggested a meeting other than those late-night walks, and oddly enough Natalie found this caution appealing. There had been too many young men expecting her to jump into bed on the flimsiest acquaintance. Both of them were busy studying for exams so their meetings were limited, and, because they were both hard up, confined to simple pleasures; taking their books and lying in the sun in the park on Sunday afternoons, walking hand in hand around art galleries, the occasional impromptu party thrown by fellow students, buying a take-away meal to eat at Daniel's place when his flatmates were out.

Perhaps it was the way they had met, Daniel galloping to her rescue like a knight on a white charger, that set the pattern for their relationship, but his protectiveness, the gentleness so touching in such a big man, reached a deep-seated need in Natalie. And Natalie's own lonely upbringing made her sensitive to the same echoes in Daniel, recognising the empty spaces inside him she longed to fill. The sexual attraction was still as dazzling, her response to his slightest touch instant and ardent, but when she would have given him all her warm and generous nature had to give she found his caring protected her even from herself.

More than five years older in age and immeasurably more in maturity, Daniel kept a rein on their lovemaking, explaining when his restraint had her shuddering with frustration, 'Darling, if you think it's not hurting me too, you're crazy! But sneaking you to bed for a hurried tumble, one ear cocked for the blokes coming back, isn't what either of us really wants. When it happens for us, it has to be *right*, and you're still very young, barely nineteen yet.'

'Too young for you?' she asked fearfully.

He gathered her into his arms, his embrace offering nothing but comfort. 'You're perfect,' he said huskily. 'Everything I've always wanted. Which is why I want to take care of you, not rush you into a heavy relationship too soon and maybe having you regret it...'

Natalie shook her head over her gullible eighteen year-old self as she unloaded the disc from the computer and locked it away safely with the others. Not so many weeks later it had been Daniel himself who was having regrets. Like his love, that tender protectiveness had been an illusion too, no longer there when she had most needed it. And certainly there had been no vestige of it in the hard man who had just interviewed her.

She cleared her desk of everything but the list Simon had asked for of the work still to be done, adding to it the extra tasks of bringing the personnel files up to date and typing up the reports on the last of the students. The only thing left was to clear the amazing number of personal belongings that had accumulated in her drawer. Luckily one of the items was a plastic carrier-bag and this was half filled when the door burst open and Simon, after one look at what she was doing, said in an appalled voice, 'Natalie, you're not *really* going! You *can't* leave me in the lurch like this!'

'You heard the man.' Natalie stuffed a handful of tissues into the bag, tearing up the empty box and tossing the pieces into the waste-bin.

'I heard him all right! I couldn't believe my ears! Well, I know I said he was a hard man, but actually he's been fine with all the other staff, courteous, even sympathetic. But the way he was with you ...' He was looking at her with expectant curiosity, as if waiting for an explanation.

But how could she explain the inexplicable? She merely shrugged and went on stuffing her belongings into the bag.

'Damn it all, Natalie, I'm not letting you go like this!' Simon's need quickly overcame his curiosity. 'You know as well as I do that I can't do your job as well as my own, *and* wind the operation up at the same time.'

'I'm sure if you ask Mr Morgan will find you another secretary from somewhere,' Natalie said unhelpfully. If she was *so* indispensable then why hadn't he raised these objections to her dismissal in front of Daniel?

Simon made an explosive sound of disgust. 'One who doesn't know A from a bull's foot! It takes months to train these girls to do half what you can do blindfolded. Natalie, please...I know that bastard was unforgivably rude to you, but don't punish me for it.'

'I'm not,' Natalie denied weakly, knowing what he said was true. Even with her list as a guide, the most efficient secretary coming in at this juncture could find herself floundering. But much as she sympathised with him she felt bound to point out, 'Simon, you're forgetting that not five minutes ago I was relieved of my job.'

'No, you weren't, not strictly speaking,' Simon came back promptly. 'Morgan was needling you into walking out, but he didn't actually sack you. In fact he doesn't have the authority to do that. He may be the great I-Am now, but *I'm* still the manager here and *I* do the hiring and firing.'

Thinking back over what Daniel had actually said, she supposed Simon was right, but even so it put her in an impossible position. 'It wouldn't work,' she said tiredly. 'If Mr Morgan's going to be hostile to my presence here...'

'But he won't *be* here, will he?' Simon said eagerly. 'He's the boss now, with the whole ca-boodle to run. Can you really see him wasting his time down here for another two weeks?'

'I suppose not,' Natalie said doubtfully. Much as she needed her job, she was reluctant to stay anywhere near Daniel's orbit.

Simon picked up that reluctance. 'Why *does* he have it in for you?' he asked curiously. And when Natalie, who was wondering that herself, made no reply, 'You knew him when you were students, you said. I noticed you called him Daniel at first, yet he's much more formal. Mrs Gilmorton every time.'

Simon had always been perceptive about people's motives. In a moment he might remember she had still been a student when she had married Hector Gilmorton, and from there leap to the conclusion that she had jilted Daniel for a richer if older man. Certainly it would provide a legitimate reason for Daniel's antagonism now—if it had really happened like that. In fact *she* was the one who had good reason to be hostile, having literally been left holding the baby.

But the last thing she wanted was for anyone around here to connect her son with Daniel, and to distract Simon from his speculations she tipped everything in the plastic bag back into her drawer.

'All right, I'll stay. If——' she wiped the pleased look from her boss's face by looking him straight in the eye '—*if*,' she reiterated, 'I can be assured of your support when Daniel Morgan tries his needling tactics again.'

Looking distinctly shamefaced, Simon hastened to assure her of it, then promptly muttered something about being needed in the staff-room and disappeared. Sighing, Natalie switched on the computer again and called up the training centre's stock control data.

Very soon the printer was spewing out the state of the kitchen stores which would have to be compared with the chef's own records when working out whether they would have enough supplies to last until the final student departed at the end of next week, and the levels of their cleaning materials and such necessities as toilet rolls and laundry on which she would have to consult with the housekeeper. Meanwhile she began to draft out a letter to be sent to each of their regular suppliers, cancelling all standing orders.

'Oh!' The surprised exclamation had Natalie's head jerking up, her mouth tightening. Today Ellen was wearing a cotton safari suit in a vivid red over a clinging white silk singlet, the effect both businesslike yet feminine, not to say dramatic, against the other woman's dark colouring. Natalie still couldn't get over the change in her.

Fleetingly she remembered the evening when Daniel had told her he was taking her to a friend's birthday party. She had expected the usual students' bash but the flat was in a more prosperous area of the city where few students could afford to live. Even more unexpected was the plump, dark-haired young woman who opened the door to them.

'Happy birthday, Ellen.' There was real affection in Daniel's greeting as he kissed her cheek then produced a small tissue-wrapped parcel from his jeans' pocket.

'Daniel! Oh, but you shouldn't have... You know we said no presents. You've got much more important things to do with your money.' The last was accompanied by an openly hostile glance at Natalie.

'It's only a little thing.' Daniel watched as she unwrapped a small glass swan. 'I thought you'd like it for your collection.'

'Oh, it's beautiful! Thank you.' The girl threw her arms around Daniel and hugged him, seeming reluctant to let him go.

Over her head he looked at Natalie with rueful apology, then, gently freeing himself, he said. 'Ellen, I've brought someone I want you to meet. Ellen Scully...Natalie Quinn. Ellen and I have been friends since we were in the children's home together,' he added. 'In fact I look on her as my *best* friend.' He didn't go on to enlarge on Natalie's place in his life, though his arm, warm and protective about her shoulders, was perhaps meant to be explanation enough.

'Certainly nobody knows him as well as I do, or has his interests more at heart.' Ellen spoke lightly but Natalie detected a warning which was re-inforced by the resentment in the dark eyes. With an airy, 'You already know everyone, don't you?' she left it to Daniel to introduce Natalie to the two other couples already there, workmates from the firm where Ellen was employed as a secretary, and their boyfriends.

She was making it obvious that Natalie's presence tonight as Daniel's partner was neither expected nor welcome, and as the evening wore on proceeded to subtly cut her out, talking of people and events Natalie knew nothing about. In Natalie's book she was being unforgivably rude. It made her wonder if Daniel had told her the truth about his relationship with Ellen. If it was really only friendship as he had claimed, then why was she behaving so jealously?

Only Daniel's refusal of a seat more comfortable than the arm of Natalie's chair and his constant attempts to change the subject and draw her back into the conversation made her stick it out, but when Ellen got him out into the kitchen on the pretext of opening another bottle of wine and kept him there for more than ten minutes Natalie had had enough.

'Thank you, but it's time I was going.' Refusing to have her glass refilled, she rose to her feet.

'Must you?' Ellen said insincerely, a gleam of satisfaction in her dark eyes. She clung to Daniel's arm, her voice softly reproachful in contrast to the challenge in her eyes. 'You're not going to drag Daniel away too, are you? On my birthday?'

'Of course not,' Natalie said stiffly. 'He's welcome to stay as long as he likes.'

'Don't be silly, Natalie,' Daniel said softly, extricating himself from Ellen's clinging hands. 'Of course I'm taking you home.'

'You'll come back?' Ellen was suddenly anxious.

'I don't think so.'

'But it's only ten o'clock!'

Natalie was surprised when Daniel pulled her into the crook of his arm so they were both facing Ellen, cutting off the others in the room. 'And we would both have been happy to stay later had you not gone out of your way to make Natalie feel uncomfortable,' he said, softly implacable, and the other girl's sallow cheeks turned a mottled red. 'Goodnight, Ellen. Enjoy the rest of your birthday.' He called goodnight to the other guests and they left.

The silence was awkward as they clattered down the stairs, but once they were out in the street Natalie stopped, facing him. 'Daniel, am I stepping on Ellen's toes?' she demanded.

'If you mean does she have any cause to be jealous of you, no, she does not!' he said explosively. 'And neither do you have cause to be jealous of her, in spite of the way she was acting tonight. Ellen and I have *never* thought about each other that way. I told you, we're friends who go way back.'

'Then why...?' Natalie said doubtfully.

He sighed, linking his fingers with hers and starting to walk. 'She's afraid you'll distract me from my work. That's what she holed me up in the kitchen for, to give me a lecture. I told her you were a student too with a career of your own to think about, and, like me, in no position to think about marriage for years yet.'

Warmed by the revelation that Daniel *was* thinking along permanent lines, albeit several years in the future, Natalie accepted his explanation. It was only later that she wondered if Daniel was wrong about Ellen's feelings for him. Certainly after that awful party she seemed to haunt them, turning up wherever they happened to be, as if making sure they rarely had the chance to be alone, nice as pie when Daniel was within earshot, cutting and acidic when he was not. And never more cutting and contemptuous as on their last meeting, her untidy hair flying in all directions, her sallow complexion mottled with anger as her dark eyes spat hatred.

Looking at the poised, sleekly groomed, sophisticated woman Ellen had become, Natalie couldn't help wondering what had wrought such a change. Perhaps it was happiness that had given her this confidence; the fulfilment of marriage that had made her realise her potential.

Natalie felt a deep envy. She wondered how long they had been married. Right from the start, when

Daniel had moved in with Ellen? Or had he made her wait to become his wife? Did they have any children?

The possibility was like a sharp knife sliding between her ribs. It was one that she hadn't allowed credence to till now, because the thought of Daniel having children by Ellen when he hadn't been prepared to acknowledge the child they had made together was too painful to contemplate.

CHAPTER FOUR

ELLEN came further into the room. 'You still here? I thought——'

'That I'd slunk away with my tail between my legs?' Raw and hurting as she was, Natalie's voice was unusually sharp. 'I have a job to do, and contrary to expectations I have no intention of walking out on it.'

'Daniel——' Ellen began, but once again Natalie cut her short.

'Simon employs me, not Daniel,' she said tightly. 'I can appreciate that you and he might find my continued presence irritating, even embarrassing, but——'

This time it was Natalie who was interrupted, not by Ellen but by a deep, clipped voice loaded with contempt. 'Irritated, perhaps, but you flatter yourself if you think I'm embarrassed, Mrs Gilmorton.'

And why should such a trivial thing as a discarded lover embarrass him? she thought bitterly, raising her head to meet Daniel's eyes across the room. Her skin prickled and her heart pounded against her breast-bone, but she refused to allow him to intimidate her, holding his gaze proudly and making her voice colourless as she asked, 'Was there something you wanted, Mr Morgan?'

He didn't speak for several long moments, his grey eyes boring into her as if trying to see what was going on inside her head. A pulse in Natalie's throat throbbed but she stood her ground and it was Daniel who looked away first as he said to Ellen, 'As it appears Mrs Gilmorton has decided against deserting her post, perhaps we could get on with our own work?' He waited for Ellen to precede him out of the room and closed the door.

Natalie let out a long breath, actually *aching* with tension. She slumped back into her chair but it was as if she had been supercharged. Her muscles just wouldn't relax.

Damn the man! What was it about him that he could still have such an effect on her, after all these years and after everything that had happened? She had left her gullible teens behind long ago yet since seeing him again she seemed to have reverted. Unless it was *because* she had been so young that Daniel had imprinted himself so ineradicably on her responses that now, even though her mind told her his treacherous betrayal had been unforgivable, his present contempt totally unjustifiable, her body re-acted independently, recognising its mate.

She made a sound of self-disgust. It was the fact that she had lived the last nine years like a nun, more like! Seeing Daniel again had merely re-minded her of the sexuality he had once stirred so effectively. Angry with herself for allowing him to get to her, she snatched up the kitchen stores printout and went to consult with the chef, throwing herself into a welter of work for the rest of the day which had the dual benefit of allowing her no time to think and keeping her out of Daniel's way.

And pedalling wearily home at six o'clock that evening she had to pull her bicycle right over to the side of the drive to allow the black Jaguar to sweep past, Daniel at the wheel and Ellen in the passenger seat beside him.

So Simon had been right. Daniel wasn't waiting around to see his instructions on the winding up of the training centre carried out. He and Ellen were already on their way back to their lives in London. She told herself she was heartily relieved and that it was the pressing problem of where she was going to find a new job that was making her feel so depressed.

When Natalie let herself into the kitchen, Kitty, keeping one eye on the fish under the grill and the other on Ginevra who was laying the table, said irritably, 'It's high time you did out the dining-room so we could go back to eating like civilised people, Natalie.'

Hector's illness had made it impossible for him to climb stairs so the dining-room had been converted into a bedroom for him, with an extra room built on to accommodate his valet and a bathroom specially designed for the disabled.

Natalie supposed Kitty was right, but, reluctant to discuss changes that the children might find upsetting just yet, she merely murmured something non-committal.

Hector had been unexpectedly good with Ginevra and Timothy after the progression of his illness had set such severe limits on his freedom. On his own admission he had been an absentee father to Ginevra in her early years, too wrapped up in the excitement of big business. And, though Natalie doubted if the actual fathering of her child had even entered his mind when he had made his extraordinary offer all those years ago, she knew he had found unexpected pleasure in participating in Timothy's development and in watching Ginevra blossom into a lovely young woman.

'You look tired, Mummy,' Ginevra observed quietly as she helped to dish up.

Natalie grimaced. 'You could say that. Poor Simon's running around like a chicken with its head cut off.'

'Do chickens run round when their heads are cut off?' Timothy asked, round-eyed.

'I've never seen it myself, but I'm told it *can* happen.' Natalie wiped a smear of salad-dressing from the end of his nose. 'What I really meant was that there's so much to be done, that we don't quite know where to start.'

'I've been thinking about what you should do when you're finally free of that place.' Kitty fixed her young sister-in-law with her eagle eye. 'You should get a good price for this house, at least enough for a deposit to put down on a flat in London. Not in a fashionable district of course, but——'

'Mummy, you're not *selling* the Lodge!'

'London? I don't want to live in *London*!'

Ginevra and Timothy both spoke at once, staring at their mother with twin expressions of horror.

Natalie was equally taken aback by her sister-in-law's assumption. 'Kitty, I have no intention of selling!' she protested. Ever since Hector had made the Lodge over to her it had represented security, a real home after all the lonely years rattling around in that great house at the top of the drive.

Her sister-in-law made a sound of exasperated disgust. 'You can't stay in this little backwater for the rest of your life! Without even a job to keep you sane? What will you *do* with yourself, for pity's sake?'

'I did think of taking an Open University course,' Natalie said, snatching at an idea that had occurred to her before.

For once Kitty looked approving, but even then she cavilled, 'I'm in full agreement with your furthering your education, but why fiddle about with a part-time course when you could go back to university and take a proper degree? And if you do it in London, I know several influential people on the——'

'And who would look after Timothy if I was studying full-time?' Natalie broke in quietly. 'Especially in London where I wouldn't know a soul. I know you're only trying to be helpful, Kitty——' Ginevra caught her eye with an expression that said her aunt was being downright interfering rather than helpful '—but my first priority is to maintain a secure, stable home for Timothy and Ginevra.'

'Very commendable, I'm sure,' Kitty said patronisingly, 'but you're talking as if that were only possible here. Surely you also owe it to the children not to become a complete rustic cabbage, as you would, mixing only with the yokels down here?'

Stung into uncharacteristic retaliation by her sister-in-law's disparaging tone, Natalie retorted sharply, 'The people of Priorsford are *not* yokels, and, anyway, I couldn't afford to move to London even if I wanted to.' Which she certainly didn't, not when it looked as if Daniel would be running the company from there.

Kitty looked taken aback to be spoken to so sharply, but was still convinced she knew what was best for everyone. 'Well, when I get back to London there'll be no harm in my making enquiries as to your chances of getting a place at the university there.'

'Why can't she mind her own business?' Ginevra muttered. 'Interfering old bat ... No, I'll see to these,' as Natalie began to clear the table. 'You go and put your feet up. And that's an order!'

She gave in gratefully, and had no sooner settled herself on the sofa than Timothy snuggled up beside her and began to tell her about his day, his small face vivid beneath his choirboy cap of blond hair. It was only then that she realised that Daniel had left without once mentioning his son, let alone troubling to enquire about his welfare.

It hurt. Far more than the hard, contemptuous attitude he now adopted towards her, more than his studied insults, this cut deeply into her heart, that Daniel had evinced no interest, not even curiosity, in this beautiful child they had made. Such indifference was totally at odds with the kind of man she had believed him to be, but then hadn't she discovered nine years ago how mistaken she had been in her estimate of his character?

They had only made love that one time. For the whole of that term she and Daniel had been content to pursue an old-fashioned courtship. Well, not exactly content. There had been many times when, stirred almost beyond bearing, Daniel had returned Natalie to the hostel to toss and turn restless with frustration in her lonely bed while he quenched his own fires with a cold shower.

But then the term was over and a parting of the ways loomed over them. Natalie was to go home to Priorscombe and the possibility of a summer job at a hotel in Sidmouth while Daniel looked for a labouring job to swell his savings before he moved to London to start the vocational training that would follow his law degree. Suddenly his promise of all the time in the world carried less conviction.

They sat in the pub on the fringe of the end-of-term celebration, too much unhappiness weighing them down to be part of the conviviality.

'You will come down to Devon?' Natalie asked anxiously. 'Even if you can only manage the odd weekend?'

'You're sure it'll be all right?' The grip of his hand tightened on hers. 'I wouldn't want to——'

'Of course it will; there's plenty of room,' she assured him quickly. 'Please, Daniel. I can't bear the thought of leaving tomorrow not knowing when I'm going to see you again. Or even if...' she added miserably.

'Oh, lord...don't talk like that.' His instinctive protest was almost drowned out by a burst of raucous laughter. 'Hell! I can't stand any more of this. Come on.' He pulled her to her feet, hurrying her back to his empty flat where they fell desperately into each other's arms.

The rest had been inevitable.

Natalie shook her head sadly over the romantic, naïve little girl she had once been even as she listened with half an ear to her son's chatter. On Daniel's narrow, rumpled bed she had experienced fulfilment for the first—the *only* time in her life, and together they had created this beautiful child.

Not that such a possibility had occurred to her at the time. She had still been floating on her rosy cloud when Daniel groaned, 'Oh, hell, Natalie, you should have stopped me. I shouldn't have——'

Natalie covered his mouth with loving fingers, stopping the words. 'I wanted it too, Daniel. And it was...' she paused, searching to describe the indescribable '...wonderful, fantastic, stupendous.' Her eyes glowed like purple pansies. 'All of those but so much more. Utterly amazing, in fact.'

But Daniel still had a troubled pleat between his brows. 'It was the first time for you, wasn't it?'

'Of course. There's never been anyone else and now there never will be.' Her earlier shyness forgotten, she trailed her fingertips over the golden whorls of hair on his broad chest, loving this new freedom to touch him, to explore his mysteries. Lifting her gaze to his face she saw he still looked troubled. 'Does it matter that I was a virgin?'

He trapped her hand with his, his face serious. 'That depends. I take it from your attitude you *are* protected?'

'Protected?' she echoed naïvely.

'As in the Pill, or some other form of contraception?' His voice was urgent now.

That was when she had begun to come down to earth. 'Well, no. I thought...I mean, I didn't...'

She faltered to a halt as, swinging his long legs to the floor, he towered over her, angrier than she had ever seen him. 'I don't believe I'm hearing this! You let me make love to you *knowing* you could get pregnant?'

Natalie cringed, stunned by Daniel's transition from caring lover to angry accuser, too hurt to point out that *he* had been just as carried away by his emotions as she had. Her deep blue eyes darkened to slate as bewildered tears filled them, blinding her so that she didn't see him move, only felt the side of the bed depress as he sat down.

'I'm sorry. Oh, lord, please don't cry...' His sudden anger seemed to have dissipated as he clumsily wiped the tears spilling down her cheeks with his fingers. 'Natalie... I didn't mean to shout, and I certainly shouldn't be blaming you. It was *my* responsibility to make sure you were protected before... Ellen was right,' he went on bleakly. 'It *is* too soon to get into anything heavy...'

Each word crushed her further. What to her had been a unique experience, the most wonderful fulfilment of their love, he saw as a mistake, an error of judgement bitterly regretted. Yet even while her heart writhed in pain her head told her he was only being realistic. He had fought so hard, overcome so many obstacles in order to get this far along the road to becoming a barrister. To have a child to support would probably mean having to abandon that ambition.

'I don't suppose for a moment I——' she began but Daniel cut in drily,

'I wish I had your faith!'

'I was about to say that in the unlikely event of finding myself pregnant it will be *my* problem.' She lifted her chin proudly, refusing to acknowledge a *frisson* of pure fright. 'So you really don't have to worry.'

Daniel's face was a picture of indignant disgust. 'For a supposedly intelligent girl, you talk a lot of tripe, Natalie.'

'I don't see why,' she defended quickly, colour coming to her pale cheeks. 'After all, it was neither rape nor seduction, was it?'

'Exactly! We did it together,' he said grimly. 'And if there *are* any consequences we'll face those together too.'

'Mummy, you're squeezing me!' Timothy protested, wriggling.

Natalie realised she was hugging her son fiercely as she remembered the promise Daniel had never kept.

Relaxing her convulsive clasp, she ruffled his fair hair, looking lovingly into the features that were a replica of his father's. It was just as well Daniel had disappeared back to London. They didn't need him complicating their lives. He had his life with Ellen now, and, for all she knew, other children.

Natalie braced herself against a shaft of pain. This persistent harking back to what was over and done with nine years ago had got to be mastered.

It was in a very determined state of mind that she arrived at her desk the next morning. The day promised to be even busier than the previous one. By the afternoon she would have all the lecturers' reports on the students to process, so, only having the morning available to make inroads on all the extra work that was piling up, she went straight through into the adjoining office.

'Simon, did you get instructions about——?' She stopped dead in her tracks, shock suspending her breath.

'Sorry to disappoint you,' Daniel mocked. 'You'll have to make do with me.'

She had been so *sure* he had gone back to London. 'I...you...' Painfully she managed to drag air back into her lungs, but even to her own ears her voice sounded strained as she said politely, 'Thank you, no. It was Simon I needed to see.'

'Indeed.' It was a sultry day and the thin cotton dress Natalie was wearing was clinging damply to her figure after her bicycle ride up the drive. As he leaned back in his chair, his powerful shoulders straining against the material of his expensive jacket, his leisurely inspection was a studied insult. 'Didn't he tell you? Perhaps you're not that close to him after all. And I was sure he must be a second string to your bow, as it were, now your plans for me have fallen through.'

Only by an involuntary widening of her eyes did Natalie betray her shock at this fresh attack. What had she ever done to him to warrant such bitter antagonism? Quelling her puzzlement, she said quietly. 'I have no interest in what you believe, Daniel,' and watched a muscle jerk along his implacable jaw. 'Neither do I intend to discuss my private life. So, if you could tell me where I can find Simon...'

Irritatedly Daniel sat upright again, flicking his cuff to glance at the slim gold watch on his wrist. 'At this moment Chesney is well on his way to London.'

This time Natalie's pulse wasn't proof against her shock. 'He's *left*?' she said incredulously. Immediately an explanation occurred to her. 'Did you sack him because he overruled you concerning *my* dismissal?'

'No, I did not!' Daniel's grey eyes flashed as he ground out the denial between clenched teeth. For the first time she seemed to have penetrated his cold disdain to spark a flash of genuine emotion and she lowered her thick lashes to hide her satisfaction, though that was short-lived as he went on tersely, 'As a matter of fact he went at my suggestion. He's spending a few days at head office to see what the job he's been offered there entails.'

Natalie was silent for several moments before she said quietly, 'That was thoughtful of you. I'm glad Simon's not going to lose by the closure of Priorscombe. He put a great deal of work into making it a success.'

A strange expression crossed the granite hardness of Daniel's face, replaced so quickly by derision that she thought she must have been mistaken in thinking it was surprise. 'And what about you, Natalie? Are you going to lose by it? But of course you don't need to worry about being out of a job, do you? You came from money and you married money.'

She supposed it must look like that to him, but for a few moments the precariousness of her situation with no income until her husband's estate had been settled, and now no job, while still having responsibility for the upbringing of two children, brought a flash of sick panic which was reflected in her face before the downward sweep of her lashes masked her feelings.

Ignoring his jibe, she said, 'If this place has to be closed down by the end of next week, I have some queries that won't wait until Simon returns.'

When this met with no response she raised her eyes to see a deep frown drawing his strongly marked brows together. It was several seconds before he seemed to realise she was waiting for a reply. 'I'm sorry?'

Natalie repeated what she'd said and, snapping out of his uncharacteristic distraction, he demanded tersely what it was she needed to know. They worked together for perhaps twenty minutes, Natalie refusing to notice the way the ray of sunlight making its way between the chimmey-pots highlighted the lighter streaks in his thick brown hair, or to appreciate the quickness of his brain and the decisiveness of his answers. The unlikely rapport was only broken when she had the temerity to ask what was going to happen to the house once the training centre had closed.

'That's *my* business,' Daniel said curtly. 'Any more questions?'

'None,' Natalie snapped back.

He stared at the tight line of her mouth broodingly. 'Just as a matter of interest, Natalie, exactly when did you decide an elderly millionaire was a better bet as a husband than an impoverished student?'

For a moment she was stunned, and then she wanted to cry aloud at the injustice of this accusation and the pleasure Daniel seemed to get out of making it. Instead she gathered up her papers and walked to the door where she paused to look back at him. 'You mean I had a choice?' she asked ironically, and had the satisfaction of seeing a dull flush crawl over his cheekbones before she slipped through the door and closed it quietly behind her.

Natalie's hands were shaking as she sat down at her desk, only now allowing the tide of burning anger to sweep over her. How *dared* he point the finger of scorn at her? As if *she* had been the one to dump him! He hadn't even had the guts to tell her to her face that he wanted out, though the writing had been on the wall if she hadn't been too besotted to see it ...

Only ten days after they had parted—she tearful, he frozen-faced—on Bristol station, Daniel had come down to Devon to see her, arriving without warning just as she and her father were finishing their silent Sunday lunch, asking for her at the kitchen door, because, as he admitted when they were alone, seeing the size of the house he had assumed her father must work there. She had been too delighted to see him to pay much attention to his shock at finding that the dingy, crumbling mansion was actually her home, throwing herself into his arms, only realising he wasn't returning her kiss with his usual enthusiasm when he broke it off to ask urgently, 'Natalie, everything *is* all right? I mean you're not ...?'

For the first time since the early days of their relationship she had felt shy with him. 'If you mean do I know if I'm pregnant or not, it's still too early to know,' she said awkwardly.

The look of dismayed frustration on his face hit her hard. She had thought a lot about their situation over the last few days, and, though on one level she couldn't believe her one experience of physical love could really lead to her pregnancy, on another level she longed for it to be so, longed to be carrying Daniel's child beneath her heart, a child that would link them together indissolubly.

'Would it really be the end of the world if I was, Daniel?' she asked, unconsciously wistful. Before he could translate the appalled expression on his face into words, she went on quickly, 'Oh, I realise it wouldn't be easy, but you'd have your grant, and I could work for most of the nine months. I'm quite a good typist.'

Daniel's derisive, 'Oh, sure, your father's going to love the idea of you married to a penniless student and living in a grotty bedsit,' was like a slap in the face.

'I told you,' she returned miserably, 'he doesn't give a damn what I do.' Her father had had his head buried in his racing paper when the housekeeper had shown Daniel in and had only acknowledged him with a grunt.

It was clear he didn't believe her. 'Even if you weren't used to all this...' His gesture encompassed all that had come as such a shock to him.

'All what?' Natalie was near to tears. Couldn't he see the place was crumbling away around her ears?

'Oh, come on, Natalie.' His voice betrayed his weary exasperation. 'Talk about the princess and the pauper! I've never even *met* anyone who actually employs a housekeeper before.'

'Daniel, living with you in the smallest attic in London would be an improvement on what I have now, as long as you love me,' she choked.

There was a momentary softening of his expression, as if she had touched a chord. 'Oh, Natalie... I know you think you mean it but, believe me, you have no conception... Your father——'

'My father wouldn't give a damn!' She had always hated this cold, comfortless, tumbledown barn of a place and the cold indifference of the man who owned it. Priorscombe had been the scene of a lot of misery in her short life, and now it was responsible for this.

'I can't believe that! Good lord, if he had any inkling that I might have made you pregnant he'd probably take a gun to me! And I wouldn't blame him for thinking I'd done it on purpose, in order to marry you for your money.'

'Money?' She gave a laugh, rough with tears. 'You don't know how funny that is! Why the hell do you think I was working in that awful bar every weekend? Because I don't *have* any money. I've *never* had any money. I'm never likely to have any money—not from my father. Shall I tell you how much he cares about me? I came home at the end of my first term at university—Christmas, mind you—to find the house locked, dark and empty. No housekeeper, no heating, not even any food, and nothing to tell me where he'd gone, or why.'

For the first time there was a crack in his certainty. 'I'm sure it must have been something important for him not to have remembered to leave a message,' he said uncertainly.

'Oh, it was important.' Natalie's irony was almost lost beneath the tears. 'He'd had a better offer from one of his horse-racing friends. I spent that Christmas at the local pub, working for my keep, and wondering all the time whether my father intended to come back at all!'

Daniel just opened and closed his mouth as if bereft of words, then, with a groan, enfolded her in his arms. 'Natalie...Oh darling, don't cry. I had no idea! I mean, who would ever have imagined——?' He broke off as an insistent hooting from the front of the house warned them his friends had finished their pub lunch in the village and were back to collect him.

'Hell! Why did they have to come back *now*?' He took several paces away from her, then came back. 'So what you're telling me is that if you *are* pregnant you can expect little support from your father?'

Natalie saw the defeat in his eyes and was appalled at her own self-centredness. What to her would be the fulfilment of her dreams, to him would mean having to give up his most cherished ambition. 'I'm sorry,' she whispered. 'Oh, Daniel, I'm so sorry. I really have messed up your life for you, haven't I?'

'Don't say that! I—— Oh, hell!' And then he was kissing her with a force and passion he had never used before and, winding her arms around his neck with a sob, she opened her mouth, responding with an equal desperation. And for maybe a full minute all the old magic was there, Daniel's heart increasing its tempo against her breasts, his arms binding her fiercely to him.

But another burst of impatient tooting had him holding her at arm's length again, veiling with thick lashes the flaring passion that burned like white flame in his light eyes. 'I must go. Look, Natalie, let's not cross our bridges, hmm? We could be worrying about nothing, you know. As long as you let me know one way or the other...?'

She nodded dumbly. And if she was pregnant? They had still not properly discussed their options, but never for a moment did she doubt that Daniel would stand by her.

And now he had the unmitigated gall to condemn her actions and despise her. Well, never again would she flinch from his contempt. Never again would she allow his snide remarks to hurt.

The threatened storm still hadn't broken and it was more sultry than ever that afternoon. Natalie had her window wide open but as it was at the bottom of a wall no more than twelve feet square and only looked out on to the bare, enclosing walls it did nothing to temper the heat. Normally on a hot day she would have had both the door into the corridor and the door to Simon's office open to allow the air to circulate better, but today her privacy was more valuable than her comfort. Her cotton dress had visible damp patches and her choirboy fringe clung to her hot skin, but she worked her way doggedly through the student reports and in the absence of interruptions—Ellen hadn't put in an appearance all day and Daniel, after glowering at her all through lunch as she sat

at the tutors' table, had left her severely alone—
the completed folders were steadily piling up.

The afternoon was well advanced when a
welcome current of air heralded the opening of the
communicating door and the much less welcome
voice of Daniel saying disgustedly, 'Good grief, how
can you work in here? It's like an oven!'

'With difficulty,' Natalie muttered through
gritted teeth, not lifting her head from the notes in
front of her.

She wished he would go, but the prickling at the
back of her neck warned her he was still hovering.
Then from the corner of her eye she saw his hand
reach out to the pile of completed folders.

'You've done all these since lunch?' he exclaimed as he flicked over the pages.

He sounded surprised and Natalie couldn't help
a touch of complacency at having vindicated
Simon's opinion of her efficiency. 'It's our normal
practice to get the student reports in the post on
Friday evening,' she said calmly, 'though this week
they'll have to wait until Monday.'

After several moments' silence Daniel said, 'All
right, I'll buy it. Why the delay this week?'

Natalie ostentatiously marked her place in her
notes and looked up. 'Because Simon always takes
the late post into Exeter, and he isn't here.'

'And, being such a conscientious secretary, you
have no thoughts of taking the job on yourself?'
There was a gleam in his eyes that told her he had
noticed her brief complacency and for a few moments she had to fight an answering spurt of
humour.

'None,' she said briskly. 'In the first place, thanks to your economy drive, I no longer have transport, and, in the second place, I'm already working late as it is, finishing these reports.'

Daniel, ignoring her jibe about his repossession of the car, moved away from the desk, but when she hoped it was to go back into his own office he paused, turning back to her. 'So why do it, Natalie?'

She blinked in surprise. 'Because it's my job, of course.'

'You misunderstand me. I mean why do *you*, Mrs Natalie Gilmorton, do it?' He advanced on her again, placing his hands on the desk, leaning towards her. 'It can't be the life you envisaged for yourself when you decided a rich *old* husband was going to be a better bet than a young poor one.'

'I didn't marry Hector for his money,' she defended, and knew at once that it had been a mistake.

His very stance was threatening, his nearness overwhelming. Natalie felt as if he was pinning her to her chair by the force of a dark emotion she couldn't understand or identify. 'Why else would you marry a man old enough to be your father—*grandfather* even? For his virility?'

Her instinct was to back away in the face of his savage contempt but pride compelled her to hold her ground. With chin raised, she said quietly, 'For his kindness, and the fact that his need was as great as mine.' But still his charge of marrying for money stung, as did his assumption, betrayed in an earlier remark, that she had come from money. It was this she was thinking of—the fact that though she had been born and brought up in this great house she'd never had anything from her father but minimum support during her childhood, not a penny of pocket-money, not even as much as a Christmas or birthday present—that prompted her to add, 'Anything I've ever had, I've *earned*.'

The anger flaring in the grey eyes so close to hers was no longer cold but searing. Deep lines were scored in his face as his mouth twisted to spit out, 'Oh, it was earned all right. In an old man's bed! And you must have leapt into it straight from mine!'

It was a cruel, tasteless jibe, intended to cause pain, voiced with a bitterness that seemed to Natalie out of context. 'I don't understand you, Daniel.' She gazed at him with puzzled blue eyes. 'Why are you so angry? It was you who walked away from me, remember, so what can any of it matter to you now?'

It seemed she had touched a raw spot, for he jerked upright, and then the tension was shattered by the peal of the telephone.

CHAPTER FIVE

BEFORE Natalie could move, Daniel's hand snaked out for the phone, his snarled, 'Yes?' enough to send the hapless caller into trauma. But as he listened some of the angry rigidity left his face.

'For you,' he said, holding out the receiver. 'Derry and Briggs, solicitors.'

She took the phone from him, catching a strange expression in his cold grey eyes, something that might have been satisfaction, before he turned and strode back into his own office, closing the door firmly behind him.

It was the secretary, telling her Mr Derry needed to see her as soon as possible. 'He doesn't usually open the office on Saturday mornings, but he knows it can be difficult for you to get into Exeter on weekdays, so if it's convenient he'll be there at ten-thirty tomorrow.'

Natalie agreed to the appointment and thanked her. It must be that Hector's estate was near settlement at last.

Her feeling of relief made it easier to put that last ugly scene with Daniel to the back of her mind, and she finished printing up the reports and preparing them for the mail without noticing the thunder rumbling round the combe. It was only when she followed her usual routine and carried them out to the entrance hall to leave them on the post table by the front door that she realised the storm had broken. Lightning flashed from a lurid sky and rain hissed down with such force that it hit the ground and bounced up again.

Natalie groaned at her lack of foresight in coming out unprepared that morning and hurried to the housekeeper's room to see if she could borrow a waterproof. But being Friday night there was no one about, not even the caretaker who saw that all the lights were off and all doors locked. Hovering by the side-entrance, she wondered if it might be sensible to wait until the storm eased off a little, but the risk of running into Daniel again made a wetting the lesser of the two evils. Slamming the door behind her, she plunged into the downpour, head bent, and though she kept as close to the wall as she could she was still soaked to the skin by the time she reached the outhouse where she kept her bicycle.

She wheeled it round to the front of the house and was just about to get on when with a swish only just audible above the hissing of the rain a black Jaguar swung in front of her and stopped, blocking her way. The door opened and Daniel sprang out, his face as thunderous as the weather. He was wearing a waterproof over his business suit and in the seconds it took him to stride round the car it was running with water.

'What the hell are you playing at?' he shouted. 'You look like a drowned rat. Get in the car. I'll take you home.'

He was already attempting to take the bicycle from her but Natalie hung on. 'Look, I'm wet through already. I'm not going to get any wetter cycling home.'

'In a storm like this? Talk sense, woman, or are you *trying* to commit suicide?' As if to underline his warning a fork of lightning zigzagged down the combe and across the drive. Almost instantaneous was the crash of thunder that had Natalie involuntarily relinquishing her grip on the handlebars. Tossing the bicycle aside into a flower-bed, Daniel gripped her arm, hurrying her to the car and pushing her inside.

Natalie watched him warily as he got in the other side. 'There's a towel on the back seat,' he said, wriggling out of his wet waterproof. 'Mop yourself up.'

She twisted round and the first thing she noticed was the pile of reports she had left in the hall. 'You're taking the post to Exeter?' she said, picking up the towel that lay on the seat beside them.

'London,' he said shortly. 'It seemed the logical thing to do.'

Of course, it was the weekend. Naturally he would be going home. Home to Ellen. She rubbed her hair vigorously.

'Is that old boneshaker your only form of transport?' His tone was derisive but that undercurrent of antagonism was still there. 'Your wealthy husband didn't buy you a car of your own?'

Natalie passed him the towel. 'As I was the family chauffeur, there was never any need for more than one car.'

Daniel paused in rubbing the wet from his own hair to look at her. 'And you haven't thought of using some of the loot you must have accumulated to buy yourself another one?'

Natalie's generous mouth compressed. 'No,' she said shortly, for she was damned if she was going to keep protesting that she hadn't married for money.

Without further comment he finished drying his hair, tossed the towel into the back and put the car into gear. He was forced to drive slowly; not only were the windscreen wipers struggling to cope with the deluge but in places the drive was in danger of becoming a second stream, running with water.

Even so, they were soon at the Lodge, its red-brick walls glistening wetly as the Jaguar drew up outside, its sheltering trees reducing the noisy drumming of the rain on the car roof. And thank heavens it *was* raining so hard, Natalie thought, reaching for the door-handle, or Timothy and perhaps Ginevra too might have come running out to greet her.

Daniel was staring at the house broodingly through the windscreen. 'So this is where you're bringing up my son,' he said, his voice heavy with bitterness. 'I suppose you leave him with some child-minder while you're working.'

Natalie's hand stilled. Indeed everything in her seemed to still, her heartbeat, the flow of blood in her veins, her power of speech, even her thought processes, as she stared at him dumbly, her eyes pansy-dark in her blanched face.

Although it had hurt her that over the several days since they had met again Daniel had never mentioned the child they had made, now he finally had she was bitterly angry. '*Your* son, Daniel?' she rounded on him, her eyes flashing her contempt.

'It takes more than being present at the conception to become a father!'

'You're surely not going to pretend Hector Gilmorton was a father to him?' He turned to look at her, bitter distaste etched deeply into his hard features. 'He soon shuffled you off to this hideaway when he finally realised you were trying to foist another man's bastard on him, didn't he?'

His words hit her like barbed darts. He thought she had seen her opportunity of deceiving a wealthy man into fathering her son, and, when she had been found out, had been incarcerated in the Lodge out of the way. No remorse for the way he had callously deserted her and the son whose existence he had apparently only just remembered in order to follow the god of his ambition. And now he had the gall to put his own twisted interpretation on her actions!

'At no time did Hector Gilmorton *ever* suffer under the delusion that my baby was his,' she said between gritted teeth. 'But he was big enough to treat him at all times as if he were. Why else would he have left Tim as well provided for as his own daughter?'

'So why did he—a millionaire—leave you only a token income?' he came back like a striking snake.

Natalie was shaken but lifted her chin proudly. 'Strangely enough, it was at my insistence. Not that I expect you to believe that.'

Daniel's smile had no vestige of humour in it but told her clearly enough what he thought of her claim. She shrugged, knowing it was useless to try to convince him of something he didn't want to believe. And once again she wondered at his hostility, as if *he* were the one to have cause for resentment.

She looked at him curiously, trying to find traces of the man she had once loved so much in the unyielding planes of his face and the contemptuous grey eyes. 'What does it matter to you anyway?' A sudden unwelcome thought struck her. 'You're surely not going to pretend an interest in my son after all this time, Daniel?'

'*Pretend* an interest!' He stared at her as if he couldn't believe his ears. 'Why, you cold-hearted, manipulative bitch! There hasn't been a day all these last nine years when I haven't thought of my son, growing up a stranger, not knowing he has a father who would have loved him given half a chance.'

'How can you *say* that?' Natalie was oblivious to the clammy discomfort of her wet clothes, outrage at the injustice of his accusation and resentment of what he was claiming coalescing into a blazing anger that blanked off any other considerations.

'What a very convenient memory you do have, Daniel,' she marvelled. 'You don't recall at all that the possibility of my being pregnant sent you into a tail-spin? Or that when I needed you most you were gone, leaving your leering, sniggering flatmates to tell me you'd dumped me?'

She turned to open the car door but before she could release the catch his hand was like a manacle round her wrist, turning her back to face his angry, 'This is the second time today you've tried to imply I deserted you, when we both know it was the other way about. Oh, I'll admit I wasn't full of enthusiasm at the possibility that you might be pregnant, but we could have worked something out if you'd only told me.'

Natalie had thought that the hurt from all those years ago was long over and done with but Daniel's spurious claims reopened the old wounds. 'And how was I supposed to tell you, Daniel?' she asked bitterly. 'By the time I knew for sure, you'd already moved out of your flat and omitted to leave a forwarding address.'

The days after Daniel's visit to Priorscombe had been fraught, and by the time nearly three weeks had passed she could no longer pretend it could be a false alarm. Between apprehension and the nausea that was to dog her throughout her pregnancy, the train journey to Bristol had been far from comfortable and had turned into a nightmare when she had reached Daniel's flat, only to be told he'd moved out a week or more ago, his former flatmates maintaining throughout her desperate questioning that they had no idea where he had gone. Their leering, half-pitying grins had shown only too clearly that they thought Daniel had ducked out of a relationship that had grown too hot for him.

'That's just not true! Within a week of coming down here to see you I wrote to tell you I was having to give up the flat and giving you a new address where you could reach me. When I didn't hear anything from you, I wrote again. And again.'

His brows were drawn together in a ferocious frown, but Natalie was in no mood to listen to his lies, cutting in furiously, 'Oh, I found your new address eventually, but not from any supposed letter. And you have the gall to accuse *me*! It was *you* who decided Ellen was a better bet because she could help you realise your ambitions while I would only be a hindrance.'

'Ellen?' The frown had faded and Natalie would have sworn his puzzlement was genuine had she not known better. 'What on earth does *she* have to do with any of this?'

She didn't know what convoluted game he was playing but she was sick of it. 'Oh, do stop pretending, Daniel,' she advised wearily. 'Ellen spelled it all out in words of one syllable when I swallowed my pride and went to see her.'

Even now, nine years later, she could still remember the numbing shock, the feeling that the world had suddenly started to spin backwards and nothing was real or recognisable any more. Had she been capable of thinking at all she might have recognised the truth then, that Daniel had callously deserted her. Instead, instinct telling her that if anyone knew what had happened to him it would be Ellen Scully, she had laid herself open to more humiliation and disillusion.

'Nothing's "happened" to him, except he's come to his senses and moved in with me.' There was scorn in Ellen's voice and a defensive hostility in her stance as Natalie faced her in the doorway of her flat.

'You mean you're putting him up for a while?' Hope was a long time dying.

'I mean we're together, period,' Ellen corrected her. 'When he moves to London in a few weeks I'll be going with him. At last he's admitted he's never going to make it with you hanging round his neck like a millstone.' She gave Natalie a sidelong glance of pure malice. 'At least with me he can be confident I won't screw everything up for him by getting pregnant.'

Natalie flinched, her pale face whitening further. 'You—you're sleeping together?' She closed her eyes but the pictures forming in her mind were imprinted behind her eyelids. Shaking her head to dislodge them she croaked, 'No, I don't believe it.'

For the first time Ellen showed anger. Grasping Natalie's wrist, she dragged her unwillingly across the sitting-room, snatching open a door and thrusting her through. 'What do you think that is, Scotch mist?' she snarled, whirling Natalie away from the double bed to face the chest of drawers piled high with Daniel's law books. 'And this?' She slid one end of the fitted wardrobe back to reveal a couple of pairs of jeans and several T-shirts and sweaters recognisably his, hanging next to Ellen's dresses.

The nausea Natalie had been struggling against for most of the day almost overwhelmed her. Perspiration beaded her clammy face and she was desperate to sit down, but the only place was the bed and she couldn't bear to go anywhere near it.

'Daniel wouldn't...he *couldn't*...besides, he said I must tell him——'

But, as if the evidence of Daniel's change of heart wasn't irrefutable enough, Ellen hammered home, 'You never really knew him if you still haven't understood what an ambitious man Daniel is, and how much he'll sacrifice to get where he wants. I'm not saying it's a particularly praiseworthy trait. Maybe you have to grow up as we did, with nothing, to admire that kind of single-minded drive. The hard truth is, Natalie, I can help him to attain his ambitions while you can only be a drag on him, holding him back.'

'I don't believe what I'm hearing!' Daniel's voice broke in on that old anguish.

But Natalie had had enough of his denials. Blue eyes flashing scorn, refusing to be intimidated by his deepening frown and grim mouth, she reached for the door-handle. 'You made your choice nine years ago, Daniel. Neither I nor my son are any concern of yours. So go home to your wife. Go back to Ellen and leave us alone.'

She slammed out of the car, too angry to notice that the rain had stopped and everywhere sparkled beneath the re-emerging sun, or to notice how shaken was the man who stared after her.

At least her soaking wet condition gave her the perfect excuse to go straight to the bathroom, for she was still shaking with reaction from her outburst and doubted she could have sustained a normal conversation with her family. She spent twenty minutes lying up to her neck in warm, scented water, giving her seething sense of injustice at Daniel's dog-in-the-manger attitude full rein. He hadn't cared a damn what happened to her when he had dumped her all those years ago, yet now he apparently felt perfectly justified in condemning her for the way she had survived without him.

Well, he could be in no doubt now what she thought of his mealy-mouthed hypocrisy! she thought with satisfaction. When she had demolished his pathetic claim of having written to her he hadn't been able to think of a thing to say in his own defence.

Drying herself vigorously, Natalie still couldn't work out what was behind Daniel's attacks on her, nor his motive in belatedly turning his attention towards Timothy. He couldn't surely be thinking of claiming any rights as Tim's natural father?

Wide-eyed she stared at her blurred reflection in the steamy mirror, the strangest feeling curling in her stomach, a mixture of panic, outrage and something else she couldn't identify. Closing her eyes briefly, she called on her not inconsiderable common sense. Why would he, after all this time? Besides, Ellen would never stand for it. She had always been obsessively possessive of Daniel. There was no way Ellen would accept Natalie's child's figuring in even a minor way in Daniel's affections. In fact, she ruminated, if she had any more trouble with Daniel it might not be a bad idea to threaten to complain to Ellen.

But hopefully she wouldn't need to. Perhaps that unpleasant little scene in his car had cleared the air and he would leave her alone. In fact once he got back to London and Ellen he could easily decide there was no need for him to come back to Priorscombe at all, not with Simon due to return on Monday to supervise the final closure of the training centre.

She might never have to see Daniel again, she thought as she wriggled into a pair of well-worn jeans and hunted through her drawer for a clean T-shirt, and was dismayed at the hollow ache that thought brought before she determinedly suppressed it. She had expended enough anguish over Daniel all those years ago. No woman in her right mind would wish it on herself a second time. Besides, there was something very distasteful about coveting another woman's husband. No, better for them all if, when he got back to London tonight, he stayed there.

The following morning both Ginevra and Timothy decided they wanted to come into Exeter with her so all three of them walked down to the Green Boy where the minibus was waiting in the car park to begin its first run of the day into Honiton, the rotund and beaming Eddie Mothersole handing them aboard with a softly burring, 'Come you on up, my 'andsomes.'

The first mile or so was along a high-banked, narrow lane, just wide enough for one vehicle, and halfway along they met the milk tanker on its collection run. It was the kind of situation that had been a nightmare for Natalie, driving her husband's big Volvo, but Eddie reversed neatly and drew into one of the passing-places, allowing the tanker to go on its way.

It was the only vehicle they met before they reached the main road where driving was less hairraising. Eddie dropped them in Honiton's bustling main street where they joined the queue for the bus, and about an hour later they were in Exeter in good time for Natalie's appointment.

Ginevra offered to take her young brother to the underground passages while their mother kept her appointment, so they parted just outside the bus station, Natalie relieved to be missing the almost obligatory visit to the claustrophobic passages that had been excavated to improve medieval Exeter's water supply and which, dry now and open to the public, held a fascination for her son.

It was cool after the previous afternoon's storm but the flowers along Southernhay, the elegant Georgian terrace where the family solicitor had his office, looked refreshed from their soaking. Alan Derry let her in himself when she rang the bell and ushered her into his office. He had an upright, almost military bearing, an impression fostered by his closely cropped dark hair, so the mischievous, mildly flirtatious hazel eyes came as something of a surprise. 'It didn't cause problems, asking you to come at such short notice?' he queried, motioning her to a chair. His father and grandfather before him had taken care of the Quinn family's legal business, though he hadn't met Natalie herself until just after her marriage to Hector Gilmorton. He had been newly qualified then, already influenced by the scurrilous stories in the Press and prepared for a heartless little gold-digger. The reality had been very far from his preconceived idea, and ever since he had found it hard to maintain a suitable professional detachment with her.

Natalie shook her head, smiling. 'If it's to hear that the estate has finally been settled I'd have gladly *walked* here. Ginevra had her letter this week. She's won her place at Oxford, so it'll be a relief to know the money's there to supplement her grant.'

Alan asked her to pass on his congratulations then shifted in his chair with uncharacteristic unease. 'I'm sorry if this request to see you raised your hopes. I *have* been pressing for a speedy settlement but you must realise your husband's estate was extensive and complicated, though this was a complication I *didn't* expect.' At her puzzled look he picked up a paper from the file in front of him. 'Natalie, I've received notification that your husband's will is to be contested.'

Natalie's jaw dropped, her eyes widening as she stared in disbelief. 'You can't be serious! *Contested!* How can it be? I mean, by whom? Not...not *Kitty*?'

Alan Derry shook his head. 'I put that badly. It's not the actual disposition of the estate that's being contested, only your nomination as the children's guardian, and it's Daniel Morgan who's bringing the action. It seems being their trustee isn't enough for him. He wants to replace you as their guardian too. *Natalie!* You're not going to faint?' Seeing her face drain of colour, he leapt from his chair, patted her shoulder helplessly then shot to a filing cabinet, taking out a bottle and slopping some of the contents into a glass before pushing the glass awkwardly into her hand.

The fumes of the neat whisky hit the back of her nose as powerfully as any smelling salts, steadying the whirling room, but Alan still looked anxious so she took a cautious sip, and the ensuing fit of coughing banished any lingering faintness.

'Why would he want to do such a thing?' she asked in bewilderment. 'More to the point, *can* he do it, Alan?'

'He means to try. This...' he indicated the document in his hands with a grimace of distaste '...is to inform us that he intends to ask the courts to have you declared an unfit person to handle the children's income.'

Shocked, Natalie slumped back in her chair, the words 'unfit person' echoing inside her head. The man who had once professed to love her, who had then deserted her, left her to bring up his son alone, was now trying to have her stigmatised as an unfit person to bring up that same son?

'But why?' She ran a hand distractedly through her hair. 'Why would he do such a thing? I'm their *mother*, for heaven's sake! Doesn't he care what effect a court case would have on the children? Obviously not. I suppose a lot of it might go over Timothy's head, but Ginevra... She's had enough upsets in her short life.'

Ginevra's plight, as a motherless little girl rattling around that great London house since her mother's death in a skiing accident, and with only paid help to look after her, had been one of the reasons why Hector had offered her marriage, and one of the reasons for prompting Natalie to accept.

Why was Daniel *doing* this? Hector's will had been specific enough, and Daniel had benefited considerably from it, inheriting shares of his own as well as the voting rights of Ginevra and Timothy's shares. Was he greedy enough to want the use of the children's incomes as well? But that would be illegal, when Hector had stipulated that she, as their guardian, should use the money for their education.

Even if Daniel had no ulterior motive, he could insist on nothing leaving the trust funds, she realised, neither capital *nor* income, until each of the children reached twenty-five. As far as Timothy was concerned it didn't worry her too much. She had always felt a little uncomfortable accepting anything on his behalf, only Hector's point that he had willingly accepted Tim as his son and that he wasn't

going to have him hurt at not being treated equally
with his sister having persuaded her to agree.

But Ginevra's case was different. She had every
right to the benefit of her father's money. Indeed,
without it her place at Oxford could be in jeopardy.
Natalie knew she couldn't let that happen.

Her voice was soft but her fine-boned jaw jutted
determinedly as she asked, 'Does Mr Morgan
specify in what way he considers me unfit?'

'The—er—arrangements you and your husband
came to on your marriage do leave you at a dis-
advantage, Natalie,' Alan said gently. 'Morgan is
saying that because your husband virtually cut you
out of his will there will always be the suspicion
that you will administer the children's fortunes to
your own benefit and not theirs.'

Natalie drew in a sharp breath at the insult.
'Hector *didn't* cut me out.'

The solicitor shook his head irritably. 'It's what
it looks like to other people, Natalie.' He had always
considered her scruples over benefiting from her
husband's wealth foolishly quixotic. 'Oh, yes, *I*
know your husband was complying with your
wishes, but to someone who doesn't know the
facts . . .'

Natalie's quick brain grasped the point immediately. Oh, but it was ironic! Had she agreed to
Hector leaving her the considerable fortune that had
been his original intention, Daniel wouldn't have
been able to make his insulting allegation. One of
the reasons for her stubborn refusal to accept anything more than a modest income from her husband's estate had been to refute the gutter Press's
innuendoes at the time of her marriage that an

eighteen-year-old girl would only tie herself up to a man forty years her senior for what she could get out of it. Now, it seemed, even that had backfired on her, giving Daniel a stick with which to beat her.

Because this was aimed at her, she was beginning to realise. His claim to be safeguarding the children's interests was just a smoke-screen. This challenge to her guardianship was meant to hurt and humiliate her. She had only to remember his other spiteful actions: repossessing her car, reducing her status as training centre secretary to casual work and denying her the right to redundancy payment, his deliberate twisting of the facts, trying to pretend it was she who had dumped *him* in favour of a wealthy older man, acting as if *he* were the injured party.

What she didn't understand was *why* he was doing it. She could have made things difficult for him nine years ago, slapped a paternity suit on him, claimed for maintenance for Timothy. But she'd done as he'd wished, bowed out of his life without a whimper. So why was he so set on persecuting her now? Unless...

It must have been as big a shock to him as it had been to her to discover that Hector had all unknowingly thrust their lives together again. He must have wondered how he was going to face her. His conscience must surely have pricked a *little*. Could his strangely bitter antagonism be his way of submerging his guilty conscience? Her brow furrowed as she followed this train of thought. Daniel couldn't have failed to read in the newspapers about her marriage to Hector so soon after his desertion; his allegation that she had leapt into an old man's bed straight from his was proof of that. And, though he had dumped her in favour of Ellen, might he still have been jealous? Maybe by now he actually *believed* his own twisted version of events!

'If only I'd known about this yesterday I could have asked him to his face what he was playing at,' she said with impotent anger.

Alan Derry sat up straight in his chair. 'He's *here*? He's actually *met* you?'

His tone implied that, having met her, Daniel Morgan couldn't surely want to pursue this threatened court case, and Natalie silently thanked him for that. 'He *was*.' She massaged her aching temples as she went on to explain, 'According to him, the UK side of the company's finances are in a mess.'

Alan Derry's eyebrows shot out of sight. 'And are they?'

Natalie shrugged. 'My sister-in-law seems to think it could be true, and it's entirely possible that towards the end Hector was too ill to hold all the threads. Anyway, Daniel Morgan was down here to tell us he's closing down the training centre to cut costs and selling Priorscombe to realise the assets. He went back to London last night. Of course he *might* be down again, but, as he's already sorted out the redeployments and redundancies, and as the training centre closes its doors next Friday, I doubt it.'

The solicitor was silent as he digested the information, then, 'This threat of legal action would have been put in train some time before he came down here. You don't think he'll want to withdraw it now he's met you?'

Natalie just wished she could have such optimism! She shook her head. 'He hasn't been . . . friendly.'

Alan's eyebrows almost disappeared again. 'And what about the children? Was he . . . unfriendly with them?'

'So far he's shown no inclination to meet them,' Natalie clipped, echoing silently, and long may it remain so!

'It's beginning to sound as if your husband's confidence in him was misplaced.' The solicitor's brows beetled frowningly as he gazed down at the document on his desk but when he lifted his head his eyes snapped with anticipation. 'We're going to fight this?'

Natalie was grateful for that 'we'. It put him firmly on her side. 'We're going to fight,' she agreed. 'To the bitter end. I don't think Daniel Morgan's going to find it as easy as he thinks to prove, in a court of law, that I'm an unfit mother.'

CHAPTER SIX

NATALIE was still seething with suppressed rage at Daniel Morgan's unbelievable nerve when they got home in the late afternoon. The Maritime Museum at Exeter was one of her favourite places with its dozens and dozens of boats of all shapes and sizes, modern and historical, and from all four corners of the earth, which visitors were at liberty to clamber over at will, but today much of its charm was lost on her.

She had done her utmost to act normally and must have succeeded as neither Ginevra nor Timothy seemed to have picked up her angry disquiet, but she hadn't been able to put Daniel and his chicanery out of her mind.

She kept remembering how he had looked when he had taken that call for her yesterday afternoon. He had known it was her solicitor and he had known what it was all about. And he had *relished* her coming humiliation! Changing out of her rather crumpled cotton dress into jeans and T-shirt, she felt the sting of tears behind her eyes. How *could* he do this . . . be so cruel and unjust? It was as if he was betraying her all over again.

Blinking the tears away angrily, she stiffened her spine, disgusted at such maudlin self-pity. She'd been through all that once on Daniel's account, had folded under his callous treatment without a word of protest. Well, not this time. She was nine years older now, hopefully a little wiser and—determinedly she squashed down the aching hurt—certainly a lot harder. Whatever the motive behind this ... this *vendetta* of his, this time she was going to stand and fight.

Which made it all the more frustrating that Daniel was no longer here to hit back at. And that was exactly as he had planned it, she thought bitterly, staring from her bedroom window up the combe towards the big house.

Preparing their evening meal, Natalie found she was missing Hector profoundly. Of course, in a way, her problems were of his making, but he had always provided a fatherly ear for her worries or frustrations, his clear, logical thinking cutting them down to size. Now she had no one to sound off to or to ask for advice. Kitty was hardly a kindred spirit, and anyway she had spent the afternoon doing the church flowers—or rather directing the village ladies who worked on a rota—and was too full of righteous indignation at their lack of gratitude to even remember that Natalie had had an appointment with her solicitor, and Ginevra was too young.

The feeling of alienation was still strong in her when she arrived at work on the Monday morning, having had to walk because her bicycle was still in the flower-bed where Daniel had thrown it when he had forced her into his car. She found Simon was back, and so full of the new job he would have at head office that Natalie wanted to scream instead of putting her 'ooh's and 'aah's in at the right places.

She was glad there was plenty of work to keep her occupied, sitting in on the technical reps' conference to take notes, and when five o'clock brought their first day's formal discussions to a close Natalie still had all the notes to type up.

She had been at it for an hour or more, absorbed in the task, when a touch on her shoulder had her head jerking round to look straight into Daniel Morgan's silver-grey eyes. '*You!*' she gasped, her heart beating wildly.

'Why so shocked?' he mocked. 'You knew I'd be back.' The silvery grey eyes held the same relishing expression she had seen before.

'To gloat?' she said contemptuously. 'Yes, that would be in character.' Then the angry frustration she had been bottling up ever since her interview with the solicitor exploded and she shot to her feet with such force that he actually retreated a couple of steps. 'How *dare* you try to label me as an unfit mother? *You*, the man who deserted his son before he was born!'

Daniel took a step forward, his face dark with anger. 'I did *not*——'

'I know what you did!' Natalie was too angry herself to be intimidated. 'You didn't care what happened to Tim then, so don't pretend you care now. You gave up all rights to him when you dumped me for Ellen, so if you think I'm letting you or your wife anywhere near——'

'Ellen Wheeler has nothing to do with any of this,' he broke in, 'so you can cut the raging. It's a good act, but——'

'*Wheeler?*' Natalie had heard nothing further. 'She's not...' Her laugh had a wild note of hysteria. 'You mean you deserted her too? Oh, Daniel, *not* a very good record for a man who's trying to get guardianship of my children.'

She gave a yelp as Daniel grabbed her shoulders, shaking her ferociously before slamming her against his body and swooping to capture her parted lips. His kiss—if it could be called that—was as ferocious as his shaking had been, straining her neck at a painful angle, stopping her breath, forcing her lips against her teeth until she could taste blood. When he released her her knees buckled and she would have fallen had he not pushed her into a chair.

'I'm sorry.' His hands were shaking as he passed her a handkerchief to stem the trickle of blood from her split lip. 'But it seemed the only way to stop your lies. Did you really think I wouldn't check on your story? Of course I went to Ellen with your accusation. She was thunderstruck.'

'You're going to tell me she denied it.' Her lip felt twice its usual size and it was painful to speak. 'Well, of course she would if you told her to. You may not have married her but she'd still perjure herself for you.' Even as far as standing up in court and lying for him? She suddenly felt very cold.

'If anyone's perjuring herself it's you, Natalie,' he retorted savagely. 'Or have you begun to actually believe your little fiction in order to justify yourself? Why not be honest for once? You saw your opportunity for an easy life and married your rich old man.' He made a gesture of disgust. 'Money marries money. I should have realised as soon as I saw your home. I *did*, and then fell for your sob story about your father not caring. No doubt he whistled up your elderly suitor when he realised you could be getting in a bit deep with a penniless student.'

The very real bitterness twisting his mouth bewildered her. He sounded as if he really *believed* what he was saying. And if he was a good enough actor to make *her* begin to doubt what she knew to be the true facts, just how easy would he find it to sway a judge with his fiction?

A wave of desolation swept over her, mirrored in her pinched features. That it could be *Daniel* . . . 'Why are you doing this to me?' she whispered, her blue eyes deadened with hurt, her mouth held stiffly to contain the pain. For just a moment there was a softening of his forbidding expression, until she went on, 'What have I ever done to you that you should lie and cheat in order to hurt me?'

'You can ask me that?' His face was pale, a muscle jerking in his jaw, his eyes a frozen wasteland. 'You gave my son to that old man! Hurt you? I could kill you for that, Natalie. Well, just as you gave me no choices nine years ago, I'm giving you no choices now. I want my son. If you fight me I'll reduce you to nothing. I've already been successful in delaying the settlement of your husband's will; my application to contest for the guardianship of the children will delay things even more, and by the time you do get the payout I'll have run you so deeply into debt with lawyers' fees that it'll take all that income for years to come. Yes, you might well look stricken. It's time for *you* to start paying now.'

A creeping coldness held Natalie immobile, a coldness that began as an icy breath shivering her skin, then spreading deeper to slow the flow of blood through her veins, then deeper still to the core of her. She wasn't even aware of Daniel slamming out of the room, though she sat like a statue staring at the door long after it had shuddered to behind him.

She didn't know she was in shock, only that she had never felt so cold in her life, or so sick with fear and helplessness. Against all sense and reason, Daniel's threat echoed and re-echoed around her mind, growing like some monstrous thing, feeding on her many insecurities.

And gradually one threat rosè above all the rest until her shock turned to panic. 'I want my son,' Daniel had said. She had no idea how long she had been sitting there, or where Daniel had gone when he had slammed out, but supposing...

Leaping to her feet, careless of her uncompleted work still strewn across her desk, she flew out of the office. There was no sign of the black Jaguar as she collected her bicycle, which only increased her panic. The fact that it wasn't parked outside the Lodge either hardly lessened her fear; only the sight of Timothy sitting at the kitchen table, happily eating his dinner, brought such a wave of relief that she sagged against the door-jamb.

'You were so late that we decided not to wait,' Kitty reproved. 'Yours is in the oven and if it's dried up you've only yourself to blame. Surely there's no real need to work these hours? I——'

'Mum, are you all right?' Ginevra broke in. 'You look awfully flushed.'

Natalie found the strength to push herself away from the door-jamb. 'I'm just rather hot,' she said, hoping the tremor in her voice wouldn't be noticed, 'and not in the best of tempers.' She couldn't help herself crossing to Timothy, placing a hand on his bony young shoulder while she dropped a kiss on the top of his head. She squeezed her daughter's shoulder too. 'Hi, Ginny. Thanks for keeping my dinner hot, Kitty.'

'You'd better have a shower to cool off.' Kitty was still disapproving.

It was probably the quickest shower Natalie had ever taken; with Daniel's threat still resounding in her ears she was reluctant to let Timothy out of her sight.

Inconceivable, surely, that Daniel would snatch his son, yet it was equally inconceivable that he should have made the threats he had. She *had* to take them seriously. While she pushed her meal around her plate in the pretence of eating, she tried to divine Daniel's intentions from the things he'd said. If she fought him for the guardianship of the children, he was going to reduce her to poverty. The idea of being driven so deeply into debt was terrifying. But if she won then wouldn't it be worth it? Presumably then Daniel would have to give up any right in Timothy's future. Would she win, though, she wondered uneasily, if Ellen was prepared to tell lies to back up Daniel's story? Between them they could brand her publicly as the cold-hearted, mercenary bitch he was already making her out to be. She shivered. He would hardly need to point out that financially he was so much better able to care for his son than Natalie for the court to make a decision in his favour. And if she didn't fight him? As Timothy's legal guardian he would have the right to make all the decisions as to his upbringing, even to deciding where he should live, and with whom.

It was dawning on her slowly that she would lose Timothy either way if Daniel persisted in his course. Not able to swallow past the hard lump of fear in her chest, she pushed her plate away. It wasn't all fear either; there was a grievous hurt that was worse than when Daniel had abandoned her all those years ago. She had loved him desperately, and loving him had had some understanding of his dilemma.

He could still stir her, she admitted reluctantly, but there was obviously no feeling left on his part when he could so unjustifiably attack her this way.

'You've hardly touched your dinner,' Kitty accused. 'What's the matter? Are you ill?'

Natalie shook her head. The truth might have to come out eventually, but the last thing she needed now was one of Kitty's disapproving lectures, and certainly she wanted none of Daniel Morgan's threats to come out in front of the children. 'Just a bit of a headache. What I need is some fresh air.' And, because she wanted Timothy under her eyes, she added, 'How about if we catch a few minnows, Tim?'

He leapt at the suggestion and led the way to the stream that ran along the bottom of their garden.

The ground was still a little soft after Friday's storm but Natalie didn't mind the mud as she sat on the bank dabbling her bare feet in the swollen stream. She was in charge of the jam jar while her son, the water well over his knees, waded with his fishing net in search of unwary sticklebacks and minnows.

'Another one...another one...' He splashed excitedly towards her, carefully transferring the inch-long, wildly wriggling minnow into the jar to join his earlier captives. 'That's six,' he said gleefully, holding the jar up to count. 'Bet you couldn't catch as many.'

Natalie rose to the challenge, taking over the net while Timothy waded beside her, peering down at the gravelly bottom, exclaiming excitedly at each shadowy dart. Which was probably why they didn't hear the car, let alone the soft footfall over the grass.

Her first intimation that they were no longer alone was a horribly familiar voice saying, 'I've seen some sights in my time...'

Timothy, facing in the right direction, looked up curiously, but Natalie spun round, forgetting she was calf-deep in a fast-running stream and teetering dangerously.

'Careful!' As he stood on the bank too far away to reach, the alarm on Daniel's face was mirrored in her own for the few seconds it took to regain her balance.

She began to wade towards him, her first instinct to have firm ground beneath her feet, but she had not counted on his automatically gripping her hand to pull her up on to the bank. 'What are you doing here?' The shock of his sudden appearance put a note of panic in her voice as she snatched her hand out of his grasp.

The uncompromising cleft chin lifted challengingly. 'Meeting my son...at last.'

Face blanching, Natalie darted a glance at the small boy splashing towards them through the water.

'It's all right, I made sure he wouldn't hear,' Daniel said sardonically. 'I've enough sense to wait for the right time and place.' Then, raising his voice, 'So what is it you're after? Tadpoles?'

'*Tadpoles!* In the *summer*?' Timothy gave him a pitying look then added in an accusing tone, 'Mum was just scooping out the *biggest* stickleback when you made her jump.'

'Sorry.' Daniel looked suitably contrite. 'You'll have to put it down to ignorance. I've never done any fishing, you see.'

'Haven't you?' Silver-grey gaze met identical silver-grey, one incredulous, the other with an expression that defied description. Natalie watched them, rigid with tension.

'I've always lived in a city,' Daniel explained. 'Streams are pretty scarce in cities. Where there are any, they're piped underground and no good for fishing in.'

Timothy nodded. 'You could have a go now, if you like. I'd show you what to do.'

'Darling, Mr Morgan's much too busy,' Natalie said quickly, wanting Daniel gone. 'Besides, he's hardly dressed for paddling about in streams!' He had discarded his jacket and tie but she cast a derisive glance at the expensive dark pin-striped trousers.

But he was already bending to pull off his shoes and socks and the next minute was rolling those immaculately creased trousers up to his knees and taking the fishing net the widely grinning Timothy was holding out.

As he took it Daniel said, 'If you're going to be my teacher, you'd better tell me your name.'

Natalie could see her son liked the idea of being the teacher. 'I'm Tim,' he said.

'And I'm Daniel Morgan.' The man reached for his hand and gravely shook it.

'That's funny,' the child marvelled. 'That's my name too: Timothy Daniel Gilmorton.'

Daniel flashed a searing glance at Natalie, who stood tense in every muscle. 'Then we Daniels must stick together,' he said to the boy, and, stepping into the stream, 'now how about introducing me to the delights of fishing?'

Natalie could do nothing but watch helplessly from the bank as he splashed about with every evidence of enjoyment, soon getting the hang of manipulating the long-handled net and quickly adding several minnows to the jam jar.

'What do we do with them now?' he asked, holding the jar up to count the catch.

Timothy looked at his mother. 'I could keep them in my room.'

Natalie shook her head. 'You know the rules, Tim. Fish go back into the water.'

'Just for tonight...' he wheedled.

'And what about all the Mummy and Daddy fish in there wondering where their babies are?'

Daniel's ironic glance brought a sudden flood of colour to her cheeks. Had he really wondered about his son as he had claimed?

'Fish lay eggs, so they wouldn't know which of the babies were theirs,' Timothy said with unanswerable logic.

Accustomed to her son's reasoned arguments, Natalie tried another tack. 'And how would you like to be imprisoned in a jam jar all night with no food?'

'I could feed them before I go to sleep.'

'What with? Do you know what they eat? I mean, imagine being hungry and someone giving you slugs and snails to eat.'

Tim shook his head.

'And would you like to wake up in the morning and find them all dead?' She was very conscious of Daniel watching and listening to their exchange, and couldn't suppress a shiver.

Tim shook his head again and carefully emptied the jam jar back into the stream.

Daniel had seen the shiver. 'Shouldn't you be getting out of those wet clothes, Natalie?'

She was suddenly conscious that her jeans, too close-fitting to roll up for her paddle, were soaked almost to the top of her thighs and that her bare feet had collected a generous coating of mud from her scramble up the bank.

'Yes, I could do with a bath. And it's Timothy's bedtime too,' she added quickly, wanting Daniel to take the hint and go but not having much hope.

'Surely you're going to offer me a towel to dry my feet before you throw me off the premises?' The gleam in his eyes told her that he was well aware she wanted to get rid of him as quickly as possible and was enjoying thwarting her.

'Tim, darling, run up to the house and fetch a towel for Mr Morgan, would you?' It was taking a great deal of effort to conceal the stress Daniel's presence was causing her from her son, and as he ran off she demanded fiercely, 'Just why *have* you come, Daniel?'

'I told you, to meet my son.'

Natalie recognised that challenging thrust of his jaw. She'd seen it often enough in Timothy when he was digging his heels in over something. She met the challenge head-on. 'Yes, even though you've been here the best part of a week without making a move, I can understand a certain amount of curiosity. If it hadn't been for your threats, you might even have been welcome. Now you can hardly blame me for suspecting your motives.' She took a deep breath and added fiercely, 'An eight-year-old boy isn't a toy to be picked up and dropped again on a whim.'

Surprisingly, he didn't rise to the taunt. 'I know,' he said quietly. 'He's a nice kid. You've done a good job on him, Natalie.' The last was added with obvious reluctance.

'So why are you bent on making out I'm an unfit mother?' she flashed back. 'Why do you want to disrupt his life? I can't believe you're doing it out of any real concern for him.'

'What would you know about——?' He stopped. Natalie had been too absorbed in their heated discussion to notice, but they had been walking slowly across the grass towards the house. Now she saw with a sinking heart that it was Ginevra bringing the towel she had sent Timothy to fetch. And following her—Natalie closed her eyes in despair, certain she was hurtling towards disaster—was Kitty. Of course it had been inevitable that Tim would have told them about the visitor.

'I understand a towel's needed.' Ginevra, wearing very brief shorts and camisole suntop and looking, to Natalie's suddenly heightened perception, very grown up, eyed Daniel with open appreciation which he was returning with interest, not at all fazed by still having his trousers rolled up to his knees. Another man might have looked foolish, but not Daniel. Garlanded with flowers, he would still look the most masculine of men, Natalie was forced to admit—one who knew who he was and exactly where he was going.

'I'm afraid Tim persuaded Mr Morgan into the water, Ginny.' Then bowing to the inevitability of making an introduction, 'This is my daughter; Ginevra, Daniel.'

She would have said that nothing could shake his supreme self-confidence, yet, in the process of taking the towel the girl held out to him, so great was his shock that he dropped it.

Ginny laughed, bending to pick it up and handing it to him again. 'That's the reaction we get from most people,' she gurgled. 'Of course I'm her step-daughter really, but I can hardly remember my own mother.'

Kitty cleared her throat loudly, reminding Natalie that the introductions were not over yet. 'My sister-in-law, Miss Gilmorton,' she supplied reluctantly. 'This is Daniel Morgan, Kitty.'

'Miss Gilmorton.' Daniel had recovered his poise but Natalie knew a fierce satisfaction at seeing him once more disconcerted as Kitty inclined her head regally, fixing him with her most intimidating stare.

'So you're the young man my brother expected to rescue Gilmorton's. Think you can live up to his faith in you?' Before he could answer, she was going on, 'Since my brother saw fit to put you in such a position of responsibility, I do think you could have come down to make yourself known to us before now.'

Daniel recovered quickly. 'I'm sorry; less than courteous of me, I know,' he said silkily, 'but, as someone of your intelligence has obviously realised, there was a lot of urgent work for me to get to grips with in London before I could allow myself this pleasure.'

Natalie cringed at such blatant flattery, sure her sister-in-law would see through it, but Kitty was lapping it up, agreeing with something suspiciously like a simper that the health of the company naturally had to come first. 'But now you *are* here you must come in so that we can begin to get to know you, Mr Morgan. You'll want to get cleaned up and dressed first.' She cast a disapproving eye at his rolled trousers and bare feet. 'Timothy will show you to the downstairs bathroom. You too, Natalie. You'll get a chill if you don't get some dry clothes on.'

Natalie wanted desperately to protest but Kitty's basilisk stare down her commanding nose had them all doing her bidding like obedient children. Not that she wasted any time in the bathroom. On thorns over what might be said in her absence, she peeled off her wet jeans and sat on the side of the bath with her feet under the tap to wash off the

mud before drying them hastily, thrusting her legs
into a clean pair of jeans, draggging on a light jersey
instead of her splashed T-shirt and hurtling back
down the stairs just as Timothy was showing Daniel
into the sitting-room.

Ginevra bounced down the stairs behind her,
having also been banished by Kitty to dress more
respectably for their visitor. 'Gosh, Mum, you were
quick!'

Natalie couldn't prevent the heat of embarrassment rising in her cheeks. The last thing she
wanted was for any of her family to get the idea
she had any interest in Daniel. 'I didn't want to
delay Mr Morgan when he has so many other demands on his time,' she said stiffly. 'He won't want
to stay long.'

Ginevra's face fell; even Kitty, coming in with
the coffee tray, looked disappointed.

'Oh, I've nothing else planned for this evening.'
Daniel darted a triumphant glance at Natalie before
turning on a smile for Kitty and Ginevra that had
a touch of pathos in it. 'To be able to relax for an
hour or two in such attractive and peaceful sur-
roundings is as much as anyone could wish for.' He
let his glance roam appreciatively round the room,
which was filled with the golden glow of the sinking
sun.

Natalie was just marvelling at his accomplished
acting when Ginevra asked eagerly, 'Have you
eaten, Daniel? Can I get you some supper?'

Daniel said he wouldn't dream of troubling them;
he'd had a sandwich earlier in the evening, but
Kitty, giving her dire opinion of scrappy eating
habits, sent the willing Ginevra out to heat up one

of the bacon and egg pies which Natalie had baked at the weekend for the freezer.

Natalie groaned inwardly. Everyone was conspiring against her desire to have Daniel out of the house as soon as possible. The longer he stayed, the more likely it was that someone would spot the likeness between him and Timothy and start to wonder. Besides, it was dangerous, having her family like him.

But Daniel seemed intent on getting his feet under the table, figuratively speaking, praising the salad Ginevra had tossed up until the young girl glowed, begging Kitty for another cup of her delicious coffee, though his compliments to Natalie on the quality of her pie were accompanied by a slanting mockery.

'I didn't realise you were quite as grown up as you are,' he said to Ginevra. 'In fact I was very much under the impression you were still at school.'

Ginvera pinkened with pleasure, grimacing ruefully as she admitted, 'Actually I am—just. But next term I'll be going to Oxford.'

'Really!' Daniel looked suitable impressed. 'Unusual to get a holiday so close to exams, isn't it?'

'Holiday?' Ginevra looked puzzled.

It was Natalie who tumbled to what he was getting at. 'I think Mr Morgan assumes you're at boarding-school, Ginny,' she said drily, noting his frown.

'Oh, *no*.' Ginevra laughed. 'Daddy did plan for me to go but I didn't want to, and Mum managed to persuade him to let me go to her old school.'

'*Natalie* persuaded him?' He looked at her with raised eyebrows. And, whether the others were alive to his implication or not, Natalie knew he had thought she had packed her stepdaughter off to boarding-school at the earliest opportunity.

'So you all live here together, then, Miss Gilmorton,' he said, taking his refilled cup from her. 'An extended family.'

Kitty raised her eyebrows. 'Oh, this isn't my home. I've been a regular visitor since my retirement, but my home is in London, where I'll be able to return as soon as Natalie's seen sense and put this place on the market. You live in London yourself, Mr Morgan? I mean, since your return from America?' She barely gave him time to nod. 'Then I hope you'll use whatever influence you might have with Natalie to convince her that a flat there with all the job opportunities makes more sense than hanging on to this place,' she enjoined.

Natalie cringed and said quickly, 'Kitty, Mr Morgan can't have the slightest interest in whether I decide to sell up or not.'

'On the contrary.' Daniel looked at her over the rim of his cup, an expression of such grim amusement in his eyes that she wondered fearfully what was coming now. But she was as stunned as her sister-in-law when he went on, 'I'm afraid Natalie may not be able to sell the Lodge, Miss Gilmorton, at least, not yet.' He replaced his cup in the saucer with great deliberation. 'You see, your brother left a bit of a legal tangle when he made over this house to his wife. It wasn't actually his to dispose of, as it was part and parcel of the package when Gilmorton Industries acquired the Priorscombe estate. Of course I *may* still turn up a record somewhere of his having *bought* it from the company before he transferred the deeds to Natalie's name, but . . .'

Oh, but he looked and sounded so sympathetic! Only Natalie knew it was only pretence. She could *feel* his secret triumph as he struck this new blow. His threat to see her reduced to nothing had not been an empty one. Already he had thrown her out of her job and had admitted he was deliberately delaying the settlement of her husband's estate. Now he was telling her she was as good as homeless too.

CHAPTER SEVEN

'But this is dreadful! Mr Morgan, my brother could have had no idea... I suspected towards the end that he was losing his grip on things, but not *that* early on in his illness!' Kitty, in her shocked bewilderment, turned on Natalie. 'Now do you see where your stiff-necked pride has led you? If you'd allowed Hector to leave you the inheritance that was your right as his wife, it wouldn't have mattered about not owning the Lodge after all.'

'Have we got to leave here, Mum?' Timothy pressed up against her, his eyes huge, his voice anxious.

Natalie's arms gathered him in protectively as she looked with helpless frustration at Daniel. He was frowning, as if something puzzled him, but he reached out and took the boy's hand. 'No, of course not, Tim. I just meant things were in a bit of a muddle.' He looked at Ginevra and then at Kitty. 'I only mentioned it at all, Miss Gilmorton, because you spoke of Natalie selling, and that *could* have caused problems. But please don't worry. I shall do my best to sort it all out as quickly as possible.' It was only then that he allowed his glance to reach Natalie.

'If anyone can put things right, *you* can, Daniel,' Ginevra said adoringly, and Natalie threw her a sharp glance, realising that her daughter was in the throes of her first infatuation, her heart sinking still

119

further as Ginevra went on breathlessly, 'I know I told Aunt Kitty I didn't want Mum to sell, but maybe it would be fun to have a base in London when I'm home from Oxford for the vacations.' London, as the place where she was most likely to run into Daniel, had suddenly become attractive.

'Well, *I* don't want to live in London,' Timothy said truculently.

'How do you know, when you've never been there?' Ginevra dismissed.

'Because there are no streams to fish in in London; Mr Morgan said so. And I wouldn't have any friends.' His bottom lip began to quiver, though he manfully tried to stiffen it.

'Tim!' Natalie shook him gently. 'Whatever happens, we won't be going to London. I'm sorry, Ginny, but I could never afford to live there.' And the further they were from Daniel Morgan, she added silently, the safer she would feel. 'I'm like you, Tim; I much prefer the country.' She chose her words carefully, wanting to reassure him but reluctant to make any promises she might be forced to break.

Daniel surprised her by agreeing. 'I don't like living in big cities either, Tim. That's why I'm buying a house in the country myself. Of course it's much nearer to London than this is. As a matter of fact, Ginevra, it's quite handy for Oxford. You'll have to come down and stay with me, perhaps for a weekend.'

Ginevra looked ecstatic while Timothy seemed faintly envious. 'Does your house have a stream?' he demanded.

''Fraid not,' Daniel said regretfully, 'but it does have a big garden, and quite a lot of trees. As a matter of fact it occurred to me that one of those trees would be ideal for a Tarzan rope swing, if you thought you might like to visit me with your sister.'

Natalie watched the indecision reflected in her son's face. She knew what Daniel was up to. He was using his considerable powers to charm her children, to seduce them away from her, and she was helpless to counteract it. She had noticed that no invitation had been extended to her—nor did she expect it—yet if she objected to Ginevra and Timothy visiting him without her, they would see her as a spoilsport.

So she almost cheered when, after several moments' thought, Timothy said, 'We've got a big tree; the willow by the stream. You could make a Tarzan swing for me there.'

There was a small silence, as if Daniel was startled by such perspicacity in one so young, then he laughed. 'Sure, Tim, I'll put a swing in your tree. I'll get the caretaker up at Priorscombe to find me some rope. How about if I come round tomorrow night to fix it?'

Natalie was the only one not to look pleased. Tim was positively incandescent. 'Gosh, thanks, Mr Morgan!'

'Why don't you stay and have dinner with us too?' Ginevra suggested eagerly. 'The least we can do for you in return is feed you.'

Kitty immediately seconded the invitation and Daniel accepted gracefully, glancing with malicious amusement at Natalie's expression of impotent frustration. He had lost her her job, was threatening to tie her income up for years to come and was trying to make out even that her home was not her own, yet he still expected her to feed him, she thought resentfully.

Daniel asked Timothy about his school, got him to talk about what he liked doing, and Ginevra, competing for his attention, opened up more than Natalie had ever known her to before with a stranger. At last he got to his feet, thanked them for their hospitality but said he must be going. Natalie's relief was short-lived when Daniel, holding up his hand as Timothy and Ginevra stood up too, said, 'If you don't mind I'd like your mother to see me out. It was her I came to see tonight, after all.'

Ginevra looked dashed and Kitty knowing, while Natalie's cheeks burned with embarrassment at the impression he had created. Walking stiffly in front of him out of the room and across the hall, she opened the door, one question burning a hole in her mind. 'Were you telling the truth——?'

'Not here, Natalie.' He took her arm, hustling her down the path towards his car.

She could feel each fingertip, like burning brands against her bare skin. She tried to jerk away but his grip only tightened.

'Is it true that I don't have legal title to my home?' she persisted, wishing she didn't feel so aware of him. 'Or was it just another of your devious lies?'

He did let her go then, dropping his hand as if her touch contaminated him. 'I'm not the one who trades in lies, Natalie,' he clipped out. 'Oh, what your husband did wasn't actually illegal, in fact it's quite a common business ploy, and he *did* pay tax on it. But as the new head of Gilmorton Industries I am quite within my rights to question the transaction on behalf of the company.'

He even lied about not lying! 'You mean it depends entirely on your whim whether you make me homeless or not?'

'Exactly!' The grey eyes taunted her, amused at her helplessness. 'And the buyer I've found for Priorscombe is really rather keen to have the Lodge included in the deal; some religious sect who value their privacy.'

Natalie felt sick. The thought of finding herself homeless with no means of buying another was terrifying, but what really nauseated her was the cruel cat-and-mouse game Daniel was playing. 'So now you're admitting you lied to my family,' she challenged, trying to stop her mouth shaking. 'They're under the impression that you're going to save their home for them. They actually *believed* your sweet talk.'

'I merely said I'd do my best to sort things out,' he corrected. 'And I shall, though it might not be in the way they expect.'

'You were still deliberately misleading them,' she accused.

'And aren't *you* misleading them, Natalie?' he asked softly. 'You obviously haven't told them that I'm supposed to be the villain of the piece. Now I find that very curious.'

'That you're trying to oust me as their guardian, you mean? I don't consider it misleading them to try to spare them worry for as long as I can, especially Ginevra, when she's in the middle of important exams.'

He had opened the door of his expensive car, a symbol of his wealth and power and her own impotence against it. 'I grew up with my father's indifference, but it's a new experience to be so comprehensively hated,' she said bleakly. 'But, for whatever reason you've decided I've earned that hatred, please don't take it out on the children.' She hated having to plead with him, but if it saved her children any unhappiness what was her pride worth?

Daniel's brows drew together in a black frown. 'I hate what you *did*, but I don't hate you, Natalie.'

'From where I'm standing, that's very hard to believe! Especially since I've done nothing...' She broke off, rubbing her temples which were pounding with tension.

To her amazement he reached out and pulled her to him, cradling her aching head against his chest, his voice unexpectedly gentle as he chided, 'Silly woman, working yourself up into such a state. All you have to do is give in, tell me you're not going to fight me.'

At first shock held her still, and then she became aware of the heavy beating of his heart against her ear, immensely comforting. And slowly other things impinged on her senses: the strength of his arms around her, the once familiar contrast of her feminine softness and his male muscle and sinew, the heady scent of him, a mixture of clean linen, spicy aftershave and male muskiness. Mindlessly she relaxed, her arms stealing around his waist. It was all her heart had ever yearned for, to feel safe, and loved...

But it was an illusion! Daniel didn't love her. She doubted if he had ever loved her. He was doing what he had done to her family: turning on the charm to seduce her into doing what he wanted. Even so it took a considerable effort of will to draw herself away from him.

'I don't have any option but to fight you, Daniel.' There was a choked feeling in her chest and her voice was not quite steady. 'Fighting you is the only chance I have of keeping my family together. Handing over my children into your guardianship might save my home and my income, but Tim's and Ginny's happiness and well-being is more important to me than that.'

All the while she was talking, Daniel's expression was hardening again. 'And you think their happiness doesn't matter to me?' he demanded.

'No, why should it?' Natalie said bleakly. 'Tim's well-being came a poor second to your ambitions before he was born, and Ginny is the daughter of a man you apparently hated. Why should you care if she can't take up her place at Oxford?'

'What's to stop her taking up her place—providing she gets the right grades in her A Levels?' he asked sharply.

'Because she's relying on the income from her trust to live on, as her father intended.' She couldn't keep the bitterness out of her voice as she added, 'Nobody knows better than I do what trouble a girl can get into when she has to get a job to supplement her grant.'

For the first time since she had met him again, Daniel looked as if his conscience was pricking, but, too wound-up to take advantage of any softening, she rushed on, 'And how can you look after Tim properly when you have the company to run? Pack him off to boarding-school and have some house-keeper looking after him in the holidays? He's already lost the only father he's ever known, and you want to put him through the trauma of losing his mother as well! He *needs* me...' Her voice broke on a sob.

Daniel brought the flat of his hand down hard on the roof of the car without thought for the expensive coachwork. 'Damn you! Whose fault is it that I'm a stranger to my son?'

When Natalie would have protested that it wasn't hers, he flung himself into the car and slammed the door. The engine growled into life but instead of roaring off he lowered the side-window, looking at her with a face like granite. 'And to prove how much my son's well-being matters to me, I'll take you along as well if that's the only way I can have him. I'll even marry you,' he added insultingly, and drove off.

Natalie stared after the tail-lights of the car as they receded up the long drive, her silly heart still leaping. But of course he didn't mean it. It was just another move in his cat-and-mouse game. And even if he did mean it there was no way she could go along with it.

'A very personable young man,' Kitty pro-nounced when Natalie went back into the house.

And Natalie couldn't deny it. In spite of his callous betrayal in the past and his wholly unjus-tified condemnation of her now, he could still make her heart lurch in her breast. But she managed to make her, 'Do you think so?' sound so uninterested that Kitty retaliated with a snort.

'Oh, you're angry with him because he's been instrumental in losing you your job. But you know my opinion about that.' She looked at her young sister-in-law curiously. 'Doesn't the thought of moving to London and perhaps furthering your acquaintance with Daniel Morgan excite you at all? I thought he seemed quite interested in you.'

'In *Mummy*!' Ginevra exploded scathingly. 'He hardly spoke to her.'

Natalie's stomach rolled in an entirely unlooked for reaction. She didn't really think Daniel was interested in her daughter even though he had spent most of the evening winning her over, but that didn't prevent such searing jealousy at the idea that it was a physical sickness.

'He's hardly likely to be interested in a child like you.' Kitty dismissed her niece's pretensions with her usual bluntness.

'I'm not a child—I'm nearly eighteen,' Ginevra countered furiously. 'Not that much younger than Mummy was when she married Daddy.'

Before the argument could develop and end with Ginny in tears, Natalie said as a diversion, 'Considering how much you disapproved of my marriage, Kitty, you seem surprisingly keen to get me to the altar again.'

'I disapproved of your marriage to my brother,' her sister-in-law retorted.

She was saying nothing new yet Natalie couldn't help feeling hurt that after all this time Kitty had never become reconciled to her brother's second marriage, or had ever been prepared to admit that Natalie had been a good wife to him.

'A marriage to someone closer to you in age and interests would be altogether different,' Kitty went on. 'And I would have said Daniel Morgan fits the bill on both counts. It would be such a neat solution too; keeping the company in the family, as it were.'

Natalie felt mildly hysterical but before she could think of anything to say to counteract such wishful thinking Kitty was saying thoughtfully, 'You know, there was something oddly familiar about him, as if I should know him from somewhere.'

Perspiration beaded Natalie's brow. Kitty had only to take a more comprehensive look at Timothy to make the connection.

'I think if he wore his hair a bit longer he'd look like Sting,' Ginevra suggested dreamily.

Kitty looked blank but Ginny had offered a way out and Natalie seized it. 'A pop singer, Kitty,' she explained, then as casually as she was able, she added, 'He reminded me more of one of the TV news-readers.'

Kitty considered. 'Oh? Which one?'

Natalie cast about desperately. 'Can't think of his name. BBC, I think.'

'You could be right.' Kitty lost interest in the discussion, much to Natalie's relief.

'Looks as if there's been a bit of a thaw!' Simon said in a cautious undertone as the following afternoon drew to a close, and it was true that Daniel had treated her with much more consideration, if not actual friendliness. He had even paid her a compliment, asking why the time of a top-class secretary needed to be wasted when the conference notes could easily be recorded on tape.

Some of the satisfaction of having wrung that small accolade from him was dimmed by embarrassment, however, when Daniel asked, in front of Simon, what time he was to present himself at the Lodge that evening.

Only too aware of Simon's surprised curiosity, she said stiffly, 'We usually eat at six for the children, but I'm putting the meal back to seven o'clock to give you time to do that little job for Timothy first. I don't know how long it will take you, so I'll leave it to you what time you arrive.'

With the chicken casserole bubbling in the oven and the raspberry mousse in the fridge, Kitty insisted on seeing to the vegetables and taking the apricot and almond flan from the deep freeze and sent Natalie up to get ready, adding, 'I've left out some of my best bath oil for you.'

Grimacing at Kitty's obvious hint to make the best of herself for their visitor, Natalie couldn't resist soaking her tiredness away in a scented bath, or liberally sprinkling on some of her sister-in-law's matching talc. But, standing in front of her almost nun-like dressing-table, she had to squash down the rather juvenile desire to look so glamorous that Daniel woudn't be able to take his eyes off her. Not that she possessed anything glamorous anyway, she laughed at herself as she dressed again, selecting a clean pair of jeans and a plain blue shirt. After all, she would be helping Daniel to fix the swing, wouldn't she? She brushed her shining cap of hair with more than her usual vigour. Or at least watching, because there was no way she was going to give him time alone with Timothy.

There was time to check the table setting before a thump on the old iron fist door-knocker brought her heart leaping into her throat. For a few moments she froze, and Ginevra, wearing her prettiest sundress and enough make-up for her aunt to have snorted her disapproval, made the most of the time to beat her to the door. Her stomach fluttering with nerves she watched her daughter's laughing, blushing response to Daniel's greeting. Then his eyes were meeting hers over the young girl's shoulder and she was filled with a heat that made her bones feel molten and the breath catch in her throat.

He made no response to Ginevra's attempt to reclaim his attention, his eyes sliding over the blue shirt that had been a present from her sister-in-law and exactly matched the sapphire of her eyes, cut in a man's style that only accentuated her femininity, and down to the freshly washed jeans that clung to her long, slender legs and rounded hips.

It wasn't until Timothy came thundering down the stairs that the spell was broken. He slithered to a halt in front of Daniel, asking eagerly, 'Have you brought the rope?'

'Of course.' Daniel ruffled his hair before reaching behind to pick up the coil of rope he'd put down on the path. He looked at Natalie. 'Brand new, so there'll be no danger of it fraying and breaking.'

'Come on, then.' Timothy pulled impatiently at his hand.

'Can I come too?' Ginevra was feeling dashed that her mother's appearance had elicited more of Daniel's attention than her own.

'Sure.' He grinned at her. 'Though you'll have to be careful not to spoil that pretty dress. Want to supervise, Natalie? Make sure everything's safe?'

With a whoop, Timothy led the way through the sitting-room and out into the garden, running ahead across the lawn. Daniel eyed the big willow tree when they caught up. 'That branch, I think.' He pointed to one which overhung the stream, high enough to allow for a length of rope to swing right across to the other side.

'But how on earth are you going to get up there to fix it?' Natalie asked. 'We don't have a ladder.'

He looked much more like the student she remembered tonight, casually dressed in dark green cotton trousers and a silky knit shirt in a paler shade topped with a cream jacket in a soft suede. 'Climb, of course,' he said, and, giving her his jacket to hold, hoisted himself on to the first branch.

She watched with bated breath as he made his way up the tree, the rippling shoulder muscles visible beneath the clinging shirt putting forbidden memories into her mind, making her hot.

He was nearly there when Timothy shouted, 'Hey, you've forgotten the rope!' But Daniel just shook his head at them and carried on.

When he was lying full length along the big branch he had selected, he fished in his pocket and brought out a length of twine. Letting one end fall, he called, 'Tie it to one end of the rope, Tim. Tightly, now.'

The boy did as he was told, his face tense with concentration, then Daniel hauled on his end, until he could grab the rope itself. A few minutes later Timothy was joyfully trying it out, backing a couple of yards and, with a blood-curdling yodel, launching himself over the stream then letting the rope swing back with him into Daniel's arms. 'It's easy-peasy,' he boasted. 'Would you like a go?'

'Ladies first,' Daniel said. 'Perhaps your mother would like to try it.' His look of gleeful anticipation told her he either expected her to refuse or to make a fool of herself if she accepted.

Calmly she took the rope and swung herself across, her performance much more graceful than her son's, and, where he had let the rope swing him back, Natalie landed neatly on the far bank where, to their amazement, she stayed, swinging the empty rope back for Daniel to catch. She had intended him to swing it back for her to leap at, but instead he swung across himself, and before she could protest he had gathered her against him with one strong arm and was swinging back with her. The momentum of their combined weight scattered the watching group as they swung right through them and up, Daniel letting go of the rope at its highest point and landing like a cat, only to have her weight upset his balance and tumble them both on to the grass.

His actions were embarrassing enough, but when he kissed her in front of all her family before he would allow her to get up, she was scarlet with mortification.

Kitty clucked over such juvenile antics but with less than her usual asperity, and decided the dinner really wouldn't wait any longer without spoiling.

But if Natalie hoped her family would be allowed to dismiss that kiss as a momentary aberration when they got back to the house she was very much mistaken. Throughout the meal Daniel paid her such assiduous attention that she became thoroughly flustered. Kitty smiled complacently and Ginevra dispiritedly gave up trying to catch his attention for herself. Even Timothy got in on the act, inviting Daniel to come up and look at his mineral and fossil collection when it came to his bedtime.

'He's a fine boy, Natalie,' he said quietly as they closed Tim's door and started down the stairs together.

'And sharp as a tack! He must get his intelligence from you.' She was surprised that he was continuing his act when there was no one there to see, adding with a grimace, 'After all, I haven't done much with *my* life.'

'You think it doesn't take intelligence to bring up a child right?'

'Daniel, what *have* you been doing to make Mum blush like that?' Ginevra was looking up at them, holding a tray of fresh coffee, jealousy she was too inexperienced to hide in her young face.

'I was just telling her I like the way she's brought up her family, though I might have to revise my opinion if you make a habit of embarrassing her like that.' The reproof was gentle but inexorable and it was Ginevra's turn to flush fierily.

'I'm sorry, Mummy,' she said contritely. 'I didn't mean to be impertinent.'

'Of course you didn't.' Natalie smiled her forgiveness, her heart going out in sympathy to the girl experiencing her first infatuation.

After Daniel had drained his refilled coffee-cup he said, 'Much as I hate to break up a very pleasant evening, I have to make an early start for London in the morning.'

Natalie was shaken, mostly because she could have echoed Ginevra's wailing, 'You're not going back *already*?' And that was ridiculous because she should be experiencing heartfelt relief.

And Daniel had the nerve to look pleased at their reception of the news! 'Nice to think I'll be missed, but I need the early start to be sure of being back in time to take Natalie out to dinner.'

'Dinner!' Natalie and Ginevra chorused together, but in very different tones of voice.

'There's a very good hotel in Taunton,' Kitty said encouragingly. 'The food is said to be excellent.'

Daniel looked at Natalie. 'Sounds fine. You can ring up and make a booking for us tomorrow ... or anywhere else that takes your fancy.'

Natalie didn't want to go out with him. Well, she did, but not under the conditions Daniel was demanding. Perhaps that was why he had asked her in front of her family, so she would find it too embarrassing to refuse.

She was still trying frantically to think of a way out of her dilemma when Ginevra said, 'But why waste all that time driving all the way to London and back in a day? Can't you use Daddy's computer link?'

Daniel frowned. 'My secretary in London *did* mention something of the sort, but, not seeing any equipment around at Priorscombe, I suppose I forgot about it.'

'It's here, in Daddy's room. I'll show you.' Ginevra was halfway to the door when Kitty stopped her.

'I think Natalie should show Mr Morgan, Ginevra. They may need to arrange its removal back up to the big house.'

Silently Natalie led the way to the small wing that consisted of her late husband's bedroom, the adjoining room for his valet and the specially adapted bathroom which Daniel had visited briefly the night before.

Standing in the doorway, Daniel surveyed the room, taking in the high hospital bed with sides that could be raised to stop the patient falling out and the lifting gear above it, the bank of electronic equipment on a wheeled base so it could be brought close to the bed, and the table that swung across that held the keyboard.

'Explain, Natalie,' he said harshly.

'Hector had a degenerative disease.' It was the first time she had been in here since her husband's death and she was finding it more upsetting than she had expected. Blinking back the tears that threatened, she went on, 'That was the chief reason he bought Priorscombe. He knew that once his failing health was noticed around London there would be a loss of confidence in the company on the stock market and the inevitability of predators moving in for a take-over. This gadgetry...' she waved a hand towards the computers '...made it possible for him to continue running the company from here, and...' she gave him an ironic smile '...his marriage to me gave him the perfect excuse.

'Only a few of his closest colleagues ever knew the real truth,' she said when his expected comment didn't come. 'At first he was well enough to run things from an office up at Priorscombe, but there came a time when that was no longer possible, so he had the equipment brought down here. He was working right up to a few days before his death,' she finished, losing her battle against the tears welling in her eyes.

Daniel looked quite pale. 'You didn't love him,' he said. 'You *couldn't*!'

Natalie's chin came up in defiance of his anger. 'I grew to be very fond of him. He was the best friend I ever had, and I miss him terribly.'

Daniel turned away abruptly. 'Arrange to have it all moved back to Priorscombe tomorrow, will you? I'll be leaving too early to see to it myself.'

Natalie followed him out of the house and down the path to his car. 'You're still going to London, then, rather than use the computer? Are you coming back? I mean... do you still want me to book...?'

'Of course.' His smile couldn't conceal his white-hot rage. 'We've got to make this marriage of ours look credible, haven't we?'

CHAPTER EIGHT

ONCE again Natalie found herself staring at the receding tail-lights of Daniel's car in a turmoil of emotions. She had written off his ironic suggestion last night that he might even be prepared to marry her to get her son as just another twist in his incomprehensible vendetta against her, but, remembering his behaviour tonight, his kiss, his invitation to dinner, all his pointed attentions that had embarrassed her so much, she had to wonder if he had been serious.

Was that really what he had been doing? Making her family believe he was attracted to her, so that a sudden marriage between them—when as far as anyone else knew, they had only met a few days ago—wouldn't come as such a shock?

Unwilling to go in yet and face questions for which she had no answers, she made her way round the house and across the lawn to the stream. At ten o'clock on a clear June night it was still light, the sky in the west an opalescent pale green shot with pink, not even the brightest stars shining yet, though a fat golden moon hung over the trees. It was very quiet, just the chattering of the stream that never stilled, the long, eerie 'hoo-hoo-hoo' of an owl setting out on his night's hunting provoking an alarmed clatter from a sleepy blackbird, and the occasional irritable honking from a pair of wild geese who had taken up residence on the small lake at the top of the combe.

Marrying Daniel... Natalie couldn't deny her longing to be able to put the clock back, to believe in this entirely unexpected chance to realise her youthful dreams. It was still there, that powerful attraction that had drawn her to Daniel Morgan nine years ago, had been there even when he was at his most beastly to her, and she burning up with indignation, not only for his desertion of her in the past but for the cowardly way he had been trying to shift the blame on to her now.

But this was real life and dreams didn't come true just by wishing. What kind of marriage would it be—should she be foolish enough to agree—when Daniel's offer had been so insultingly made, and only because he saw it as the easiest way to get his son? How could she bear to live in those conditions with the man she had once hoped to share her life with in mutual love and trust, knowing he certainly didn't love her, knowing he despised rather than trusted her?

And could she really trust her own emotions? How could she be sure that the way he made her feel was real, and not merely the memory of a love made more poignant because she had lost it? Or, even worse, the physical itch of a woman who had been starved of a sexual outlet? No one knew better than she did the unnaturalness of the life she had been living; married, yet not a wife.

Neither she nor Daniel were the same people who had met and loved and parted so cataclysmically nine years ago. They were that much older and Natalie at least had other people whose needs must be considered now. Daniel too, perhaps? She knew nothing of his life over the last nine years. He hadn't after all married Ellen but she could hardly expect his life to be devoid of women—perhaps one special one in America? The idea twisted her gut, making her feel feverish yet at the same time goose-pimpling her skin. Jealousy, and utterly irrational too, she told herself.

She breathed deeply. Sometimes, when the wind was from the south-west, she could fancy she smelled the tang of the sea, but tonight the air was perfectly still. Concentrating on that stillness, she began to wander back across the lawn towards the house. Bedroom lights were beginning to come on along the village street. A car started up, and down at the Green Boy a wave of disco music surged as someone opened a door, and was cut off again as the door was closed.

Into the stillness came her sister-in-law's voice, calling irritably. 'Natalie? Oh, *there* you are! I was beginning to wonder what had happened to you. Brenda Mothersole's been on the phone. She asks if you can spare a few minutes to go round and see her.'

The Green Boy was more than just the village pub. Lacking a village hall as the community did, it served Priorsford as a meeting-place for the parish council, for wedding receptions and funeral wakes, for jumble sales, social evenings and Women's Institute meetings, while the skittle alley was pressed into service for disco dances and even housed the playgroup run for the few pre-school children. Thatch like beetling eyebrows over tiny windows and thick, colour-washed walls kept the rooms cool in summer and, with the help of log fires in the grates, warm in winter. Fortunately it had missed out on the passion for modernisation of the sixties, something the holiday visitors appreciated as much as the locals. The only concession to modernity were the two electronic game machines in the saloon bar, the uneven floor making them look for all the world like two slightly inebriated fat ladies leaning together for support.

Responding to the many greetings, Natalie passed through the bar and into the snug beyond. The Mothersoles had been landlords there for generations, Eddie and Brenda having recently taken over from Eddie's parents who, though officially retired, still helped when needed.

Natalie had known them all her life. They had all been at school together, she and Brenda in the same form until Brenda had left at sixteen, Eddie a few years ahead. It had been Eddie's mother Lizzie who had first started taking in holidaymakers who loved the Devon countryside but preferred to be away from the bustle of the seaside resorts, and it had been by helping Lizzie in the kitchen or waiting at table that Natalie had earned her first pocket-money.

The old pub had been her lifeline more than once in the past. Perhaps it could be again, Natalie thought with a surge of hope. In three more days she would be out of work and no prospect of any more money coming in until her battle with Daniel was won. Because to capitulate to his blackmail was a recipe for unhappiness for all of them. And in the meantime she had the children to support. As soon as she'd found out what Brenda wanted she would ask if they could do with an extra hand about the place.

Eddie and his father were behind the bar, both rotund and cheerful. Eddie poured Natalie her lemonade shandy then called for his wife. Still full of vitality after a busy day looking after her family of four children ranging in age from a year younger than Natalie's Timothy to the most recent, a babe in arms, as well as her visitors, Brenda gave a glad cry when she saw Natalie.

'I hope you don't think I've got an awful cheek, Nat, but I wanted to ask you a favour,' she said in her soft Devon burr. Taking Natalie's arm, she led her to one of the few vacant tables. 'The fact is I've just had a call from a couple wanting a room and I'm afraid I had to turn them down.'

'You're full, then?' Natalie knew Brenda's visitors tended to come back year after year.

'It's not that. I do have a room for the date they want, but she's in a wheelchair, see. Dining-room's no problem, could even hump the chair in here at a pinch, but up them twisty little stairs? No way. Then I thought of you, Nat, and them rooms of yours, ground floor, done up special for someone disabled, bathroom too.' She looked at Natalie hopefully. 'So I didn't turn them down flat, said I'd ring them back when I'd seen what you thought about putting them up for me.' Natalie tried to speak but Brenda rushed on, 'Wouldn't be any work for you. I'd send somebody over to do the cleaning. And they'd come over here for meals. You'd hardly know they were there, what with that separate entrance and all.'

Natalie had tried to break in again but her friend had obviously thought all her arguments out and she had to wait until Brenda paused for breath before she could say, 'I think it's a wonderful idea. Of course I'll have them.' She held up her hand as her friend threatened to overwhelm her with thanks. 'And if you'll let me do the cleaning for them I'll be even better pleased. In fact I was going to ask you if you needed any help here at the pub. I'm going to be out of a job on Friday, remember.'

'But I thought...' Brenda looked stunned. 'I mean...that it didn't matter, you having no job. Your husband must've...well, you must be pretty well off.' She looked embarrassed.

'It looks as if the income Hector left me could be tied up for some time yet,' Natalie said quietly. 'So I've got to get a job of some sort, and working for you would save me travelling expenses.'

'You really mean it, don't you?' Brenda looked worried. 'Well, you know I can always use a bit of extra help, but it doesn't seem right, having you working at the pub. Tell you what, use it as a stop-gap, and, if something better turns up, well, I can usually find enough casual labour.'

'You're on,' Natalie said promptly. 'And if you get any more enquiries from disabled people... There is just one thing, though. Don't book any too far ahead. I don't know how much longer I shall be at the Lodge.'

'You're *leaving*!' Brenda looked staggered.

'I might have to.' Natalie bit her lip and decided to be frank. 'The man my husband left in charge of Gilmorton Industries is trying to prove that I don't own the Lodge after all, that it still belongs to the company.'

'What? Not that nice Mr Morgan!'

It was Natalie's turn to be staggered. 'You've met him?'

'He's been in a couple of times, once just for a drink and once for a meal. He even asked if he could stay here, but of course I had to tell him I was full...unfortunately.' Brenda gave a comic grimace of regret. 'He's a *dish*! Quite made my heart go pit-a-pat.'

You and me both, Natalie thought crossly. It seemed it wasn't only her family he was putting himself out to charm.

'And you say he's trying to put you out of the Lodge?' Brenda sounded reluctant to believe it of the man who had made such a favourable impression on her, but then concern for her friend took over. 'But where will you go, Nat?'

'Lord knows!' For a few moments Natalie felt weighed down by her problems. It wouldn't be so bad if she only had herself to think about but when she was responsible for Timothy and Ginevra too... Sometimes she still found it hard to take that it was *Daniel* of all people who was running this vendetta against her.

'You could come and stay here, after the season,' Brenda offered. 'But you know I'm fully booked up to the end of September. I could get Eddie moving on the loft over the garages. We were intending to turn it into a holiday flat anyway, but you'd be welcome to it for as long as you needed it. Only even that's going to take time, isn't it? Oooh! I wish I *had* had the room to put that man

up. I'd have been able to give him an earful, treating
you like that! And to think I was actually *glad* for
your sake, a dishy man like that coming into your
life!'

Natalie was so touched, tears pricked at her eyes.
'You're a good friend, Brenda. But you mustn't
worry about me. Maybe Daniel Morgan will change
his mind.' She didn't think that likely, nor was she
about to tell her friend of the solution Daniel
himself had come up with.

To her surprise, a couple of men turned up at the
Lodge the following morning to collect the elec-
tronic equipment from her husband's room, and
Daniel was with them.

'I—I thought you were setting off early for
London this morning,' she said as she let them in.

'I changed my mind. With the computer set up
at Priorscombe I'll save both time and money.'
Something in his silvery grey eyes as they raked her
from top to toe had Natalie pulling the lapels of
the thin cotton dressing-gown she was wearing
together with both hands, heated blood leaping in
her veins.

Then the look was doused as if a light had been
switched off. Curtly he directed the two men with
him to the wing Natalie's husband had occupied
and said in an angry undertone to Natalie, 'For
heaven's sake go and get dressed!'

Feeling like a chastised child, Natalie hurried upstairs, and then was angry with herself not only for
hurrying to do his bidding but for actually feeling
guilty. This was still her home, for goodness' sake—
until he proved otherwise.

All three men and the equipment had disappeared in the van they had brought by the time Natalie came downstairs again, and all morning Daniel was closeted with the computer in the office Hector Gilmorton had once used.

Simon had already gone for lunch and Natalie was just finishing what she was doing before going for her own when Daniel stuck his head round the door. 'You've remembered to make that booking at the Taunton hotel for tonight, Natalie?'

'Well, no. I—I forgot,' she claimed, her colour flaring, but the fact was she had been hoping *he* would have forgotten about it.

His ironic look said he recognised the lie. 'Never mind, I'll do it myself. Where's the directory?'

She lifted it from the shelf, but instead of handing it to him said hesitantly, 'Daniel . . . does if *have* to be that hotel in Taunton?'

'What have you got against it?' His eyes narrowed. 'I suppose it was somewhere you used to go with your husband, and you——'

Natalie was already shaking her head. 'No, nothing like that...' Looking embarrassed, she had to confess she had nothing suitable to wear to such an up-market establishment.

Daniel was openly disbelieving. 'Oh, come on. You were married to a millionaire! You must have been there, and to places like it, many times before.'

Natalie was getting tired of his persistent misconception of the life she had led since her days as a student had been abruptly curtailed. 'I was married to a sick man, remember,' she told him quietly. 'Even if we could find places that could accommodate his wheelchair, Hector was very self-conscious about having to be helped with his food. Apart from the occasional trip to the pub, we never did any socialising, so I've had no need of dressy clothes.'

Daniel let out a long breath, looking baffled. 'All right, if Taunton's out, where else would you suggest?'

Natalie found the number of a place in Exeter she had always thought looked attractive, though she'd never actually been there. She just hoped it would meet the stringent standards Daniel had obviously acquired over the years.

By the time she got home from work she found she was feeling quite ridiculously nervous, like the callowest schoolgirl on her first date. Once again her sister-in-law offered the use of her best bath oil, and when Natalie reached her bedroom it was to find Ginevra had apparently forgiven her for being the one Daniel had asked out to dinner, for she had laid out some of her own make-up on Natalie's admittedly sparse dressing-table.

Her hands shook as she set about the almost forgotten art of applying eyeshadow and mascara, and, when Ginevra came to tell her she was doing it all wrong and insisting on supervising a new application, Natalie began to feel like a pedigree dog being groomed for Cruft's. The unexciting sapphire-blue cotton dress she slipped into rather spoilt the glamorous effect her daughter had no doubt been aiming at as the black lace inserts hadn't come through the frequent washings any too well.

Ginevra obviously had the same thought, demanding, 'Haven't you got anything better than that?' and going to riffle through the wardrobe, eyeing the contents with disfavour. 'I must have at least twice as many things as you, Mum. Don't you like shopping for clothes?'

'I've never had the time.' Natalie was struggling with the fastener of a rather nice string of pearls her husband had given her which she hoped would hide the worst of the worn lace round the neck of the dress. 'Besides, when would I have the occasion to wear them?'

'Looks as if you're going to now,' Ginevra reminded her a shade sulkily, and watched with interest as the colour flared in her mother's cheeks. 'Well, at least you smell scrumptious,' she added consolingly as Natalie picked up a hand-knitted shawl in case it grew cool later.

Daniel was well on time to collect her, his penetrating gaze making her even more conscious that her appearance left a lot to be desired against his beautifully cut suit—light biscuit this time—and crisp shirt. As he was tucking her into the passenger seat of his car she said defensively, 'You can see now why I didn't want to go to Taunton. This is the dressiest thing I possess.'

He shrugged. 'I only suggested it on your sister-in-law's recommendation. And because I assumed you'd be used to the best. The place is immaterial to me so I'm sure I'll be happy with your choice.'

The restaurant was in one of Exeter's oldest hotels, not far from the cathedral, and though Daniel had had to mind his head against the low-beamed ceiling the atmosphere spoke of a tradition of cheerful and informal service that had continued down the centuries.

Natalie's glowing face as the waiter settled them at their table was due partly to the sheer novelty of being taken out to dinner and partly to the still almost unbelievable fact that it was *Daniel* sitting on the other side of the small table smiling rather bewilderedly at her excitement.

She studied the menu, finding it difficult to decide, and when Daniel suggested they might share a Châteaubriand she agreed without having the least idea what it would be.

He made his selection from the wine list and it wasn't until the waiter had departed with their order that he suddenly asked, 'You can take red wine? I mean, it doesn't upset you, bring on migraine, or even...' he grinned, '...gout?'

Natalie gave a splutter of amusement. 'I've never had any so I don't know. But I'm willing to take the risk.'

Daniel looked astonished. *'Never?'*

She supposed it would be astonishing to a man like Daniel. He had come a long way since their brief courtship nine years ago. It wasn't just the expensive suit that sat so well across his broad shoulders and spoke of wealth as well as taste, it was the bone-deep confidence experience and success had laid on him like a patina. Of course a man of his sophistication would be amazed that a woman of twenty-seven could make such a confession, and she felt obliged to explain, 'Hector was strictly forbidden alcohol so we never kept any in the house—except a bottle of sherry for Kitty's visits.' And before that her father had jealously guarded the bottle of claret he had been in the habit of consuming with his dinner.

'I did have some champagne once,' she said, but thought better of mentioning that it had been to celebrate her marriage to Hector. And then, in case Daniel thought she was angling for champagne now, she added, 'To be truthful I found it disappointing, and it gave me a headache.'

Daniel was looking at her with a very strange expression, shaking his head.

Sapphire eyes wary, she asked, 'What's the matter?'

'Nothing,' he said quickly.

Colour flared in her cheeks and she wished she'd kept her silly, gauche comments to herself. Tilting her chin she said, 'I do realise I'm not as ... sophisticated as your usual dinner companions.'

'That's not what I——' He broke off as the waiter brought their first course: avocado and prawns for Natalie and rollmop herrings for Daniel. When he had sampled the wine and the waiter had filled both glasses and departed, he said mockingly, 'And what would you know of my usual dinner companions?'

Natalie had the feeling that was not what he had started to say before the waiter interrupted. 'Nothing, of course,' she said quietly. She didn't *want* to know anything about the women he had amused himself with since he had deserted her. Ridiculously, the thought of him with other women was deeply upsetting.

Whether any of this showed in her face, or not, she was surprised when he reached out to touch her hand. 'I'm sorry. It seems we both have some pretty deeply ingrained misapprehensions about each other.'

Natalie's eyes widened as she stared at him. Did that mean there had been *no* other women? And what misapprehensions did he have about her?

She continued to wonder as he said, 'You haven't tried your wine yet. Taste it. If you don't like it I'll get you something else.'

Obediently Natalie picked up her glass and sipped. The colour wasn't unlike the blackcurrant drink Timothy was so fond of, but there the similarity ended. The unexpected dryness made her blink, but then as she swallowed it seemed to spread warmth right through her. She took another sip and, prepared for the dryness this time, was able to appreciate the fruity richness. 'I like it!'

Daniel laughed. 'Don't sound so surprised.'

The Châteaubriand turned out to be a whole beef fillet cooked in a rich sauce which the waiter sliced from a serving trolley beside their table, and Natalie closed her eyes blissfully as the first bite melted in her mouth. When she was on her second glass of wine she found herself asking, 'Didn't Ellen's husband mind her coming back to England with you?'

Daniel's hand stilled with his fork halfway to his mouth. 'Back to *England*! What on earth are you talking about? She never left.'

Confused, Natalie stuttered, 'I—I'm sorry. I assumed she must have gone to America with you and had been working for you all these years.' Certainly Ellen's easy familiarity with Daniel had spoken of a long and close association, and, married to someone else or not, she had been every bit as possessive of him as she had been in the old days. Even to the extent of being prepared to lie for him, she reminded herself.

'We kept in touch, of course,' Daniel said stiffly. 'Mostly just a card at Christmas after she married, but I did write and let her know I was coming home. She came to see me, told me the job she had wasn't stretching her and asked if I had an opening for her.' A defensive note crept into his voice. 'I've already told you I found things here in a mess, so I took her on as my PA.'

Natalie digested this in silence. She was remembering back nine years and Ellen's jealous insistence that Daniel had turned to her because she could help him achieve his ambitions, whereas Natalie would only drag him down. If he hadn't taken Ellen to America with him, he must have dumped her too, yet she didn't apparently bear him any grudge. So why *hadn't* Daniel gone on to become a barrister? What could have happened to make him decide to turn to company law instead, to bury his pride and accept the help his 'Mr Moneybags' had offered?

She wanted to voice these questions but she was too cowardly. She was enjoying too much being the centre of his—mostly—approving attention and didn't want to say anything to upset things. It was dangerous, she knew, being so much aware of his attraction, and aware too that other women in the restaurant were equally fascinated by him. So she turned the conversation to books they had enjoyed, discovering that they had a number of favourite authors in common; to music, learning that they shared an enjoyment of both jazz and classical, though all Natalie's listening had been on records and videos.

She didn't want the evening to end, but inevitably came the moment when Daniel drew the car to a halt outside the Lodge.

'It was a lovely evening. Thank you, Daniel.'

'The pleasure was mine, believe me.' He switched off the ignition and got out to open her door, but the unaccustomed wine, the warmth and motion of the car, had made her drowsy and she stumbled.

Instantly his arms closed around her and Natalie's bones seemed to take on the consistency of warm candle wax. 'Oh, Daniel...' There was a tremor in her voice and the hand she reached up to touch his face wasn't quite steady either. His skin was warm and slightly bristly along the solidity of his jaw, and it was as if she was spun backwards to the time when her world had begun and ended with him. The thick twilight added to the illusion, softening the hard maturity that so often made him seen a stranger into the gentler, more vulnerable lines of the younger Daniel whom she had loved to the point of idolatry. The serious intent in his eyes made the blood surge hotly in her veins in response, while deep inside her a space that had been empty for so long was filled with warmth.

'Daniel...' Her voice was no more than a breathy whisper and even that died as his head came nearer, his mouth swooping to take hers with a gentle sweetness that was a seduction in itself. Her arms wound convulsively around his neck and the sweetness deepened to a passion that made his strong frame vibrate.

'Natalie...' He groaned her name against her mouth as if he couldn't bear to break the contact. 'Why the *hell* did you throw all this up to marry that rich old man?'

It was like falling into an ice-cold stream, and she actually gasped as if her breath had been taken. But it was at her own foolishness for allowing herself to be seduced into believing he really was as much a prisoner of that early enchantment as she was, when in reality he was still playing his devious and incomprehensible games.

And yet there seemed to be very real anguish in his face, and that confused her. She began to shake. 'I d-don't understand you, Daniel.' Her teeth were chattering too and she could hardly speak. 'Are you s-suffering from amnesia or something? I would n-never have even m-met Hector Gilmorton th-that day if you hadn't l-left me flat!'

She jerked away from him and would have fallen if he hadn't grabbed her arm. Hustling her up the path to the house, he demanded her key, and, when she seemed incapable of producing it, took her bag and found it himself. The house was in darkness except for one lamp burning in the sitting-room where Kitty had also left a tray with cups and a Thermos of coffee. Daniel pushed Natalie into a chair, holding a cup of coffee to her lips and making her drink some before pouring a cup for himself.

'I know I didn't behave very well on that last occasion I saw you,' he said, and extraordinarily there was a flush across his cheekbones. 'But seeing your home, the state you lived in... it seemed to put a chasm between us. It was as if you were suddenly another person, not the girl I thought I knew so well, and I couldn't help wondering how a girl from such a wealthy background could really love a penniless nobody like me.'

'*Wealthy!*' There was hysteria in Natalie's laugh. 'So why do you suppose I was having to work as a barmaid in that club in order to eat? You *knew* I had even less money than you when we were students. My home might have been a great house crumbling about my ears but my father only ever gave me the most grudging support—a roof over my head, food to eat, the barest necessities of clothing. Did they give you pocket-money in that orphanage you were in?'

He nodded.

'Well, that's more than *I* had. I had to earn mine, washing up and waiting on tables at the Green Boy.'

There was bafflement as well as anger in Daniel's expression. 'All right, you told me pretty much the same thing about your father nine years ago, and I accept that but ...' His tone had been almost apologetic but now his words bubbled up corrosively. 'But *still* to marry that old man, even when I'd already written to you about my plans!'

She had thought she was beginning to get through to him, and it was a bitter disappointment that he should have harkened back to his story of a letter. 'I have never, *ever* received a letter from you, Daniel,' she said tiredly. 'I only ever had the sniggers of your flatmates when they told me you'd gone and there was no forwarding address, and Ellen's crowing because you'd moved in with her. I married Hector Gilmorton,' she ploughed on when he would have spoken, 'because he offered me the only alternative when I found myself not only pregnant but homeless.'

'You father threw you out?' Daniel said incredulously.

Sighing, Natalie gripped her hands together in her lap. 'When I got home from Bristol that day, it was to find Hector Gilmorton and my father celebrating their deal. I'd never seen my father in such a good mood. He told me he'd sold up everything to Gilmorton Industries and he was using the money to buy himself a place in the South of France. He said I had a week to pack my stuff and find somewhere else to live.

'As it came on top of everything else, I was too stunned to say anything. It was Hector who asked what provision he'd made for me.' She laughed without any amusement. 'You should have seen my father's face! "She's an adult," he said. "She has her grant and she's capable of earning, or even finding some other fool man to keep her. I'm going to enjoy being unfettered with a bit of money in my pocket from now on. She'll get whatever's left when I'm dead and gone."

'It was the last straw. I'd crawled home virtually on my knees, having just learned of your desertion, screwing myself up to face my father and wondering what kind of future either I or my baby had, only to learn I no longer even had a roof, however grudgingly provided, over my head. I wasn't just hurting, I was panic-stricken. I burst into tears and blurted out that I was pregnant.'

She didn't see Daniel's expression, growing more and more grim as he listened to her recital. Although her eyes were fixed on them she didn't even see her hands writhing in her lap. She was looking down the long years and seeing that traumatic scene.

CHAPTER NINE

NATALIE'S father's fury had been almost apoplectic. 'Then you either marry the man or get rid of the brat,' he told her. 'I'm not having somebody's bastard hung around *my* neck. The deal goes ahead as planned, Gilmorton. Both I and the girl will be out of here before the end of the week.'

'But you can't treat your daughter like that!' Hector protested, horrified. 'What is she going to do, with no home and no means of support?'

'Go back to the lout who put the bun in the oven,' her father retorted crudely. 'She's been a drain on me long enough. By the time I've bought the villa and invested the rest of the money there'll be little enough for me to live on, lord knows! And that's my final word.' He forestalled any further argument by stamping out of the room.

'I'm sorry you had to be involved in all this, Mr Gilmorton.' Natalie at last found the courage to break the embarrassed silence.

'But what will you do, Natalie?' he asked worriedly. 'Will the boyfriend marry you?'

Gathering up the rags of her pride, she said, 'He couldn't even if he wanted to. He's still a student and it'll be years before he can afford a wife and family.'

'Perhaps I could help him,' Hector offered. 'But you said, "Even if he wanted to." Does that mean he's already refused to marry you?'

That touched a very raw nerve and without meaning to Natalie found herself pouring out everything that had happened that dreadful day. 'Of course I *knew* it would make things very difficult for him if I *was* pregnant,' she finished. 'But it never occurred to me he wouldn't stand by me.'

Daniel made a guttural sound in his throat, recalling her to the present. 'So that was when he offered to marry me himself,' she said, cutting her story short.

'And you agreed? Just like that?' His voice grated with incredulity, and something else—jealousy?

'No, of course I didn't.' Natalie was equally scathing. 'I couldn't believe he meant it at first. I hardly knew him. Oh, I remembered him quite well from when I was small. I'd looked on him as a kind of uncle. But I'd seen him only rarely since my mother died. He was my father's contemporary, so the idea of marrying him was ludicrous. More than that, unfair as well. Unfair to him, I mean. It seemed all the sacrifices would be on his side and all the benefits on mine, particularly when he stressed that the marriage would be platonic.'

Daniel looked at her sharply, searchingly, but said nothing.

'And then he took me to see his little daughter.' Tenderness softened her mouth as she remembered. 'Such a quiet, withdrawn little girl, about the same age as I'd been myself when I lost *my* mother. Hector's first wife had been killed in a skiing accident more than a year earlier,' she added by way of explanation.

'Anyway, Hector pointed out that he needed me as much as I needed him. More so, in fact, because then he told me in strict confidence that he had recently been diagnosed as suffering from an incurable degenerative illness and couldn't expect to live more than two or three years. Which meant Ginevra would still be a child and alone in the world, except for his sister Kitty, when he died. He said that if I would become mother and guardian to little Ginevra it would far outweigh his providing a home and support for me and accepting my baby as his own.

'It was his most convincing argument, but still I couldn't quite bring myself to burn my boats. I still couldn't really believe you didn't care what happened to me, you see, so I wrote to you—at Ellen's address. It was when there was still no reply after another three weeks that I said "yes" to Hector.'

'There was no reply because that was a letter *I* never received,' Daniel said grimly.

Her first thought was that he was lying, but then she realised there could be another explanation. 'I suppose Ellen could have thought you didn't want to hear from me,' she said carefully.

Daniel muttered something about too many damn letters going astray to be credible, and paced across the room to the window, looking out across the darkened garden. At last he turned, his face set in such lines of determination that it was impossible to tell what he was thinking. 'I really don't know whether I can believe your story or not, but it hardly matters now. This time you're going to marry *me* and just as soon as I can get a special licence.'

At first indignant at his refusal to accept her account of what had really happened all those years ago, she was then incredulous at this third, and most insistent yet, suggestion that their marriage was the only solution to their predicament. He was doing it for Timothy, of course. Silly to let that hurt, yet it did, so much that she could only protest weakly, 'But you can't want to marry me, Daniel. You don't—you don't *know* me.'

'I want my son,' he said harshly, confirming her judgement of his motives. 'I want him to know me as his father, not as some nebulous figure on the periphery of his life, and the only way I'll achieve that is if we marry and become a real family.'

A real family! Natalie thought with hopeless irony. But then Daniel had never known anything even approaching family life, so how could he know that marrying her in order to get Timothy wouldn't automatically make them a family? There had to be love, and trust. Daniel didn't love her, and Natalie doubted if she would ever be able to trust him.

Shaking her head she said slowly, 'I can accept that Timothy as a half-grown boy has more appeal for you than he did as a baby, but marrying me just to get him...Daniel, I've had experience of a—a token marriage forced on me by circumstances. Believe me, there has to be a better answer than that.'

'There is. A marriage in every sense of the word. I'm not too old, or too sick, to make sure you share my bed.' Though his mouth curved in amusement, his voice carried an undertone of mockery.

Natalie had to moisten suddenly dry lips as pictures of sharing his bed unwound in her mind's eye like a film, so vivid that she didn't see how he couldn't be aware of them too. To dispel them she said desperately, 'But there must have been other women...or rather, a particular woman, one who has every reason to expect *she* will help you found your family.'

'There have been women, of course,' he admitted, and Natalie had to school her features into a careful blank to cover the bitter sense of betrayal she knew she had no right to feel. 'I'm no monk, and as you'd jettisoned me to marry money... But I never made any of them any promises, or even led them to believe I might.'

He took her hands in a strong clasp. 'As for only wanting you for Timothy's sake...you must know it's more than that. Of course I want to get to know him, to learn to love him and have him know and love me. But that's a cerebral objective, of the mind as much as of the emotions, while with you...' his hands slid up her arms to grip her shoulders, his eyes mesmerising her, as with a thickened voice he went on '...it's a need that tears my gut. I don't know whether I love you or hate you, but I want you, Natalie, in my home and in my bed, tied to me by every possible means.'

'Daniel...' Just saying his name seemed to take all the breath she had. Everything in her responded to his need, every longing the years had suppressed tapped by the touch of his skin on hers, the strength of his arms as they closed around her, swinging her emotions round again like a weather-vane in a high wind.

Whatever Daniel's feelings for her, she knew now she had never recovered from that early enchantment herself. She wanted desperately to throw caution away, to snatch at everything he appeared to be offering. But she was no longer a naïve young girl confusing desire with love, too head over heels herself to question whether her feelings were genuinely returned. And to be married to Daniel without having the certainty of his love would be more than she could bear.

She was about to draw back from his arms, tell him she couldn't fall in with his plans, when a sound from the doorway had them both turning guiltily. There stood Timothy, his pyjama trousers slipping off his narrow hips, his fair hair rumpled, staring at Daniel truculently. 'You were kissing my mummy,' he accused.

'Now, Timothy, come out of there. You mustn't go where you're not wanted.' To Natalie's dismay, Kitty had followed her son down the stairs, a mind-boggling apparition, her quilted red dressing-gown adding to her impressive size, her grey hair hanging around her shoulders.

Natalie closed her eyes, hoping when she opened them they would all have gone away, Daniel included, but of course they hadn't, and, not wanting Kitty to raise the spectre of jealousy between her son and his father with her well-meaning words, she said, 'Of course Tim's wanted if he needs me. Mr Morgan was just going.'

Timothy came to stand in front of the man who was making no move to go, who, in fact, hunkered down on his haunches to bring himself to the boy's level. 'Yes,' he said, 'I was kissing your mother. I expect I'll be kissing her a lot when we're married.'

'*Daniel* . . .' Natalie said despairingly, but Kitty was already offering her pleased congratulations.

'You're going to live with us?' Tim stared into the man's face in front of him, his gaze finally fixing on the cleft in Daniel's chin. 'I've got one of those,' he said, fingering first his own and then Daniel's chin. Natalie stood frozen with apprehension, her heartbeat thudding in her ears, but even so she was unprepared when Tim said, 'Are you my real father? Is that why you're going to marry Mummy?'

Daniel met Natalie's appalled glance before returning his full attention to his son. 'What do you know about your real father, Tim?' he asked carefully.

Timothy rubbed one foot against his other leg. 'Nothing,' he muttered. And then, as if reciting something long committed to memory, 'Daddy told me my real father hadn't been able to look after me, so *he'd* had the great honour of being my daddy.'

While Daniel shot a searing glance at Natalie, Timothy fiddled with his pyjama cord. 'My daddy was nice. He helped me with my reading an' he was ever so good at sums and puzzles, an' finding me things to do when I was bored.' He paused, then looked up into Daniel's face again. 'But I think I'd like having a father who can fix Tarzan swings and play football with me.'

Natalie saw Daniel swallow hard, and his voice was still uneven as he said, 'And I'm going to love having a son I can do those things with. *My* son.' His hands clasped the boy's shoulders and Timothy submitted to being held close.

A long sigh behind her reminded Natalie that her sister-in-law had been a witness to all this. Appalled, she turned, but, instead of the diatribe about deceit she was expecting, astonishingly Kitty was smiling.

'You *knew*?' Natalie whispered.

'I haven't lost my faculties yet, Natalie,' she snapped at her apprehensive young sister-in-law, but her usual acerbic tone was most wonderfully tempered by that smile. 'Something rang a bell the first time I saw Daniel, but you successfully put me off the scent. Not for long, though. I only had to see the two of them putting up that Tarzan swing together to realise Daniel had to be Timothy's father. Tell me, did Hector know? Was that why he groomed Daniel to take over the company?'

'*No!*' Natalie's appalled denial was swift. That was what Daniel had accused her of almost as soon as they had met again, only he suspected *her* of having manipulated her husband. 'No,' she denied again. 'He couldn't have known. I only ever told him Tim's father was still a student and couldn't possibly afford to marry me. I never mentioned his name... *ever*!'

'Plenty of ways he could have found out, my dear...' Kitty patted her arm '...without you telling him. A private detective talking to your fellow students to find out who you'd been going around with that term? Hector always took an interest in you.'

'But I hardly knew him,' Natalie protested. 'Until he came to Priorscombe to clinch his deal with my father, I hadn't seen him since my mother died!'

'He saw you twice after your mother died,' Kitty contradicted, 'but then he had to stop because that frightful father of yours was reading more into his concern about you than was really there.'

At Natalie's blank expression Kitty explained, with touching gentleness for someone who was usually such a martinet, 'Hector was in love with your mother, Natalie, and she, I think, with him. But she was brought up in the old school; marriage vows were meant to be kept. And then there was you. Your father had never shown the slightest interest in you—you were only a girl, after all—but she knew if she did walk out on her marriage she would never be allowed to take you with her. Hector tried to keep seeing you for your mother's sake after she died, but then your father began making snide remarks about whose child you actually were ... so he had to pull back, try to look after your interests from a distance, which was why he dealt with your father over the sale of Priorscombe himself, trying to make sure provision was made for you.'

Natalie had listened in stunned amazement. It explained Hector's consistently fatherly attitude towards her, but ... She moistened her dry lips. 'And whose child *was* I?'

'My God!' The soft expletive was drawn from Daniel who, though talking to Tim to distract him from the conversation, had been listening himself.

'Your father's, of course!' Kitty shook her head impatiently. 'Good lord! Natalie, I wouldn't just have disapproved of my brother marrying you if I'd had any doubts; I'd have prevented it. Hector didn't meet your mother until you were more than a year old.'

Natalie sagged. Of course. And if she *had* been his daughter, Hector wouldn't have needed to marry her in order to take her in.

'Anyway, I disapproved of the marriage on *your* behalf, Natalie, not my brother's,' Kitty went on. 'At first I thought he was reliving his old love for your mother through you, and I thought that was unforgivable of him. When I realised it was nothing like that, that his attitude was strictly a fatherly one, I still didn't think it was fair on you.'

When Natalie tried to protest she insisted, 'My brother was *using* you, Natalie. Oh, I knew he wasn't expecting to live anything like as long as the nine years you've served, but even now you're still far too young to have the responsibility for Ginevra dumped on you. At least you've got someone to share that responsibility now. Whether my brother knew of your past association with Daniel or not, Natalie, I'm sure he would have been pleased with the outcome.'

'But I——' Natalie tried once more to protest about being railroaded into a marriage she was sure would be a disaster, but her sister-in-law ignored her.

'That is, young man,' she said, turning her attention to Daniel who was sitting in a chair with his son in his lap, 'I'm assuming you *are* willing to take on a teenager. Legally Ginevra may only be a stepdaughter but in fact she's as much Natalie's daughter as Timothy is her son.'

'You need have no worries on that score.' Daniel's expression, which had tensed at having Kitty Gilmorton's full battery trained on him, lightened in relief as he understood what she was saying. 'Of course I wouldn't abandon a lovely kid like Ginny. I know what it's like to have no one of your own. And after what your brother did for my son you can't really think I'd be small-minded enough to...'

Natalie hardly heard any more. After what your brother did for my son... Did Daniel really mean that? That he was actually *grateful* to Hector for giving his son a home and his name? Hope began to burgeon, but then, remembering his bitterness over her marriage in spite of the way he'd abandoned her to survive as best she could, she found it hard to believe such a change of attitude could be genuine. He'd sweet-talked his way into her family from the beginning. Just because he was allaying Kitty's fears about Ginevra's future didn't mean he'd forgiven her for making that marriage. It didn't mean he was at last willing to admit it had been his own desertion that had made that marriage necessary. And why should he not be ready to accept responsibility for Ginevra as well as Timothy when he had already put into motion court proceedings to replace her as their guardian?

No, Daniel had hurt her too much and too often for her to put any trust in him now.

'It's time this young man was back in bed,' Kitty said, as Timothy drowsed in his father's arms. 'We could *all* do with going to bed. Plenty of time tomorrow to make plans for the wedding.'

'Take all the time you like,' Natalie said a little wildly. 'But do bear in mind I haven't agreed to marry anyone yet.'

'Natalie!' Kitty tripped and stumbled on the hem of her dressing-gown, she was so astounded, then stumbled even more uncharacteristically over her words. 'But I thought it was all ... I mean, Daniel said ...'

At the same time Timothy's bottom lip quivered and tears filled his eyes. 'But I want him to come and live with us and be my *real* father!'

Daniel got to his feet lifting Tim with him. 'Don't you worry, son, your mother's tired and cranky. She'll be better in the morning, so why don't you let Aunt Kitty put you back to bed?' And to Kitty, 'I'll talk some sense into her.'

Natalie fulminated silently until the door closed behind her sister-in-law and son, then she hissed angrily, 'So you're going to talk "sense" into me, are you? Well, let me tell you I'm *cranky* enough not to let myself get involved in any more of your devious machinations. And don't laugh at me!' It was anger that was bringing tears into her eyes, she told herself, and not the fact that Daniel was holding all she had ever dreamed of just out of reach without giving her any hope of ever realising those dreams.

'Now, just calm down, Natalie, and tell me why you've decided you don't want to marry me after all.' He had wiped the laughter from his face but it still danced in his eyes.

'Calm down!' She paced across the floor. 'How do you expect me to be calm when you're moving us all around like chess pieces on a board, and crediting us with no more feelings? And I haven't decided I'm not going to marry you after all.'

'Thank goodness for that!' Daniel slipped in quickly. 'I was beginning to get worried.'

'The day I see anything worry you, I'll put the flags out,' Natalie snapped back. 'And you needn't pretend to misunderstand me, either. I said I haven't decided not to marry you after all, because I've never once agreed to marry you in the first place. It was *you* who announced it to all and sundry, trying to manipulate me into falling in with your plans.'

'I don't call our son all and sundry,' he defended, no amusement at all in evidence now. 'He had to know some time.'

'And Kitty,' she reminded him. 'Raising their expectations. You had no right to tell them I was going to marry you when you didn't have my agreement.'

'All right, so I used the situation to give you a push,' he admitted, 'but I was tired of you dragging your feet. I——'

'Dragging my feet?' Natalie repeated furiously. 'You were the one who told me, in the most insulting terms possible, that you were prepared to marry me in order to get Tim, but when have I ever given you reason to suppose I'd be willing?'

Dark colour ran over his hard cheekbones. 'Not in as many words, perhaps,' he said, and she blushed, remembering that more than once he had made her forget her doubts about him in his arms. Pressing home his advantage he said coaxingly, 'Oh, come on, Natalie. Admit you're outnumbered. Your sister-in-law approves, Timothy wants it, lord knows *I* want it, and so do you, if you're honest. Yes, you do,' he insisted as she shook her head, pulling away from the hand shackling her wrist. 'I can feel your pulse going like a steam hammer. You want me, and I'll prove it to you.'

He gathered her into his arms, lifting her feet right off the ground, his mouth taking possession of hers like a man starved of everything needed to make life tolerable. She tried to fight him but his arms were bound so tightly about her that there was no room to struggle, and, breathing in the scent of his skin, Natalie found herself responding helplessly, her fingers tangling in his hair as she tasted his lips and his tongue and drowned in the sweetness, while he seemed intent on drawing the very soul from her body.

'No one...no other woman has ever made me feel this,' he said against her mouth before covering her face with tiny, intoxicating kisses, and Natalie only had time to wonder briefly about those other women before he had captured her mouth again, driving every thought but her growing need out of her head.

'You see?' There was a triumphant note in his voice as he let her slide slowly down his body against his arousal. 'You want me, so let's have no more denials. We'll get married as soon as I can arrange it.'

It was that note of triumph that cut the chains of her bewitchment. *'No!'* Natalie thrust away from him, bitterly hurt by his blatant use of his sexuality in order to subdue her and ashamed of letting herself be seduced by it yet again. But she had her feet back on the ground now and if she didn't want to find herself trapped into a lifetime of such sexual manipulation she had better make sure they stayed there.

Daniel swayed from the force of her thrust until he regained his balance. 'All right,' he said, 'I'll give you more time if you insist. Until Ginevra's finished her exams.'

Natalie closed her eyes. She was very tired, and even more weary of fighting Daniel's seemingly inexorable will. She shook her head. 'I don't need time, and if you took me here on the sitting-room carpet and got my full co-operation it still wouldn't make any difference to the way I feel. I don't want to marry you, Daniel.' It was incredibly hard to actually say the words because she would have given anything to marry him if there had been love on both sides. It was the *kind* of marriage he was proposing that she wasn't able to face, loving him so hopelessly and knowing she meant no more to him than a means of getting to his son, always wondering if, once the novelty had worn off, Daniel might get tired of being a father and slide out of his responsibilities as he had once before.

Daniel's face was grave in the lamplight, showing no emotion, no sign that he had even heard her except for a muscle jumping on the line of his jaw. His lips hardly moved as he ground out, 'Why?'

She had to call on her last reserves of energy to answer him. 'I've made one marriage for my son, I'm not about to do it again. When . . . *if* I ever get married again, it will be to a man who loves me. A man I can trust.'

'And you can't trust me because you think I walked out on you last time?'

Natalie's shoulders sagged. Even now he had to qualify it with that 'think'.

'No,' she said, 'not because you walked out on me last time. I was hurt and frightened, naturally enough, but my pregnancy was as much my fault as yours, so I had no right to expect you to tie yourself to me if you'd discovered your feelings didn't go as deeply as you thought. I can't trust you because even now you're not admitting you were responsible for the way we split up. How *could* I trust a man who tries to twist the facts to make out everything was *my* fault?'

Daniel, who had been listening to her like a man carved from stone, opened his mouth as if to deny her reasoning then closed it again. The silence dragged out, heavy with hopelessness, then at last he said harshly, 'Go to bed, Natalie—you look wiped out. I'll let myself out.' At the door he paused. 'But don't think this is the end of it. We'll talk again tomorrow.'

CHAPTER TEN

BUT Daniel's threat of pursuing the argument the following day proved an empty one, because he was no longer at Priorscombe.

Natalie had fallen into an exhausted sleep as soon as she got to bed, only to wake after a couple of hours to lie tossing and turning for what remained of the night, going over and over the events of the evening. Timothy's arrival on the scene last night had been disastrous, but Daniel's involvement of him to try to back her into a corner had been unforgivable. It just went to prove how ruthless he was prepared to be to gain his own ends, how untrustworthy.

But oh, how she wished things were different! The mutual recognition of Daniel and Timothy should have been a moment for rejoicing and Daniel had turned it into another lever to blackmail her with.

She tried to get her mind off the treadmill of her conflicting feelings about Daniel by thinking of Kitty's revelation concerning Hector's love for her own mother, but though it explained what she had always felt to be Hector's astounding offer of marriage to give a young girl he hardly knew a home and her baby a name it wasn't long before she was worrying again about what the morning was going to bring, what she was going to say to Timothy, and what new pressures Daniel was going to bring to bear. For she wasn't at all sure she would have the strength of will to stand up to him again, especially if he used his dazzling sexuality.

And as it happened she needn't have worried on either count. When Natalie came down to breakfast Ginevra said peevishly, 'It seems I missed all the fun last night.'

'She doesn't believe me,' Timothy complained. 'About Mr Morgan being my real father, I mean.'

'It's true, then?' And when Natalie nodded Ginevra looked near to tears. 'And I suppose when he wouldn't marry you you decided to marry Daddy instead,' she said nastily.

Natalie guessed the news had bruised her daughter's girlish dreams, and, hurting, she was hitting back, but her heart sank. Not content with seducing her son, now it seemed he had succeeded in alienating Ginevra from her.

'Ginevra!' Kitty said sharply. 'Please don't pass comments on something you know damn all about. If anyone has reason to be thankful Natalie *did* marry your father, it's you. Now, let's hear no more about it. Your mother will tell you anything you need to know when she's good and ready.'

Ginevra had the grace to look ashamed and Natalie found herself in the odd position of feeling grateful to her sister-in-law; even more so when, as if nothing untoward had happened, Kitty kept up a flow of small talk right through breakfast.

Thankfully there was no sign of Daniel when Natalie reached her office and she assumed he was once more conducting the business of the company through the computer link. It wasn't until he didn't put in an appearance at lunchtime either that she asked Simon—casually, she hoped—if their new boss was working through lunch.

Simon looked surprised. 'He's gone back to London. Got me up at first light to tell me he was off. Didn't you know?'

A yawning hollow opening up in the pit of her stomach, Natalie shook her head.

'Oh. Thought you were getting quite thick with him.' He paused, but, when Natalie made no comment, said with a lop-sided grin, 'I must have been mistaken. I suppose, having opened up this can of worms, he knew he wouldn't be welcome presiding over the wake.' He went on to talk about the farewell party they were putting on the following day before everyone departed for the last time but Natalie barely listened, pushing food that suddenly seemed unappetising around her plate.

So Daniel had changed his mind about making another attempt to get her to marry him. He had given up. She should be breathing a sigh of relief. She ought to be glad she had finally convinced him. So why did she feel like crying? Why did she feel ... bereft, as if he had betrayed her all over again?

Had she been wrong to stand out so strongly against his proposal? Marrying him would have given Timothy the father he had a right to, and living together in a family atmosphere would at least have given her a chance of re-igniting the feelings he had once had for her. He might have learned to love her again.

Yet how could she re-ignite something that had never really been there? Daniel could never have loved her to have dropped her so callously. Oh, she could understand how disastrous marrying her nine years ago would have been for him, but if he had had any real feeling for her he could have let her down more gently. And how could she hope he might come to love her now, when he was showing such a callous disregard for her feelings with his campaign to humiliate and discredit her, with his threats of weaning her son from her by one means or another?

A campaign he could still be waging, she realised with a convulsive shiver. He had given up the idea of marrying her in order to get Timothy, but that didn't mean he was giving up his battle in the courts. He had changed tactics again, that was all.

And once again, she thought with a spurt of sick anger, he had left her to clear up the mess he had left behind. He had told Tim he was going to marry her, told him he was his father—now he had walked out without a word, just as he had before Tim was born. What on earth was she going to tell her family? What was she going to tell her son?

The day dragged but still it seemed too soon when Natalie put her bicycle away in the garage and pushed open the kitchen door. She had hardly closed it behind her before Tim said disappointedly, 'Hasn't he come with you? My—my father, I mean? I wanted to show him a card trick I learned today. Terry Banks knows lots of card tricks. I hope he comes before I have to go to bed.'

'I'm sorry, Tim, he—Daniel won't be coming tonight,' she said gently, hating to see her son's crestfallen face. How *could* she tell him the father he had just discovered wouldn't be coming back at all? 'He—he had to go back to London today,' she prevaricated.

'But he *will* be coming back here?' Timothy asked after a small silence and with such uncertainty that Natalie could have wept.

'Of course he will,' Kitty said with great conviction. 'A blind man could see he was tickled pink to meet his son at last. You don't think he's going to go away and leave you now, do you?'

Timothy's face brightened and Natalie didn't have the heart to contradict her sister-in-law. Perhaps, as the days passed, time would blunt the pain of Daniel's absence for Tim and he would eventually be able to forget that brief meeting.

And then it was Friday, the day the Priorscombe training centre would close its doors for the last time. Natalie was kept busy all morning clearing up, throwing out files that were no longer needed, packing others to transfer to head office in London.

At lunchtime it was almost a festive atmosphere. The bar did a roaring trade and the chef had put on a special menu. Everyone joined in: students, lecturers, cleaners, maintenance staff and kitchen workers. There were many expressions of regret that the training centre was closing and promises to keep in touch, but there was also an air of optimism among those staff members who next week would be taking up new positions within the company and looking forward to new challenges, Simon among them.

When, at half-past two, the taxis began to arrive to take people to the station, the party wound down quickly. Too low-spirited to take part in the cheerful leave-taking, Natalie went back to her office where she still had the final students' reports to print out before she too would be able to leave.

Simon found her there. 'Doesn't seem right, somehow, taking off and leaving you still working,' he said guiltily.

'You've got a long journey, and these won't take me more than an hour,' she assured him.

'Yes, well.' Her former boss shuffled his feet. 'I just wanted to say I'm sorry we shan't be working together any longer, Natalie. And I—er—wanted to give you this, a thank-you for putting up with me all these years and for taking a lot of weight off my shoulders.' He produced a small box which, when Natalie opened it, revealed a silver brooch of two hands clasped in friendship which she recognised as the work of a craftsman silversmith from Honiton.

'Oh, Simon, it's lovely! Thank you, I shall always treasure it.' She was so touched that tears flooded her eyes.

'Don't, for heaven's sake, cry, or you'll have me in tears too,' he joked to cover the emotional moment. 'I hope things go well with you, Natalie. Take care.'

'You too, Simon.' She reached up to kiss his cheek. 'Goodbye. Safe journey.'

She let the tears flow for a while after he had gone, then settled down to finish her work. The printer was chattering away so that she heard no footsteps, the tall figure looming in the doorway so unexpectedly that she jumped in alarm.

'I'm later than I intended and I was afraid you'd have gone with the rest,' Daniel said, coming right into the room, 'but I might have known you'd still be working.'

Confused, she stared at him, her heart beating wildly. Shock at his sudden appearance, she told herself firmly, lifting her chin. 'I didn't expect you back down here again.'

'Of course you did,' he denied, his expression grave enough to make Natalie feel distinctly uneasy. 'You may have thought you had the answer to everything, but I told you it wasn't the end. I've got a few answers myself now. If you can leave that, I've brought someone to see you.'

In puzzled apprehension Natalie allowed him to lead her away from the office quarters to the deserted drawing-room. Except it wasn't deserted. Ellen Scully—whom Natalie now knew to be Ellen Wheeler—stood there, immaculately turned out but gripping the back of a chair so tightly that her hands looked bloodless. Natalie's apprehension intensified, for experience had taught her that where Ellen was, trouble followed. Feeling slightly sick she squared her shoulders to meet whatever was coming.

Surprisingly it was Daniel who spoke first. 'Ellen has something to say to you, Natalie.' And when the other girl merely looked sulky, 'Don't you, Ellen?' he prompted with the kind of menace in his voice that Natalie had never expected to hear him use to his long-time friend.

Ellen licked her lips then muttered grudgingly, 'Daniel dragged me down here to tell you I lied to you that day you came to my flat looking for him. He didn't think you'd believe it, coming from him. He said you had to hear it from me.'

'Lied?' Natalie repeated stupidly. Whatever she had been expecting from Ellen, it wasn't this.

'If Daniel *had* been staying with me, it wouldn't have been the way I implied.' A bitter self-derision coloured Ellen's voice. 'As it was, he never even used my sofa, let alone moved in with me. The things I showed you were just some of his belongings I was looking after while he was in America.'

The events of that day had been seared so deeply into Natalie's consciousness that all she could feel was a kind of whirling confusion. Her mouth had dried and it took two attempts before she could ask, 'You mean it was a lie, that you and Daniel were lovers?'

Ellen shrugged. 'Wishful thinking, perhaps. Of course I couldn't be sure you'd come to me when you found Daniel gone, but I hoped you might, and I was ready to take advantage of it when you did.'

Natalie drew a deep, painful breath. After a few moments' thought she said, 'But the rest . . . that he was dumping me because I was holding him back from realising his ambitions? That had to be true. How could you have hoped that I'd come to see you if you hadn't known Daniel had walked out on me?'

Ellen's mouth tightened, and the glance she darted at Daniel was rebellious. 'The whole story, Ellen,' he said grimly.

'Daniel never walked out on you, Natalie,' she said grudgingly, and Natalie wondered what threats Daniel had used to persuade her to talk. 'He wrote to tell you he was having to go to America and to give you an address where you could reach him, but I destroyed the letter. It wasn't difficult,' she added with a touch of bravado. 'I was helping him pack up at the flat and the letter was there. All I had to do was offer to post it. He trusted me, you see.'

The expression on Daniel's face reflected his pain and disgust. 'Of course I trusted you. You were the nearest thing to family I ever had.'

For all her bravado, Ellen flinched. 'And about a fortnight later I also destroyed a letter with a Devon postmark addressed to Daniel care of my flat,' she finished doggedly.

Daniel's hands clenched into fists and for one awful minute Natalie thought he was going to lash out at Ellen, but then she saw him flex his fingers as if consciously restraining himself. 'I wonder if I ever really knew you, Ellen.' He thumped the back of the sofa. 'What in the world possessed you? *Why* did you take it upon yourself to play God?'

Ellen's chin came up. 'I was jealous, of course. There you were, throwing away any chance of becoming a barrister, and for that pretty little *useless* doll! I'd have happily gone out to work to support you through your pupilage and until you'd got a start and were beginning to earn yourself, but you never even looked at me.'

'My God!' Daniel looked really shaken. 'And I never suspected!' He looked at Natalie. 'I even accused you of having a fixation about Ellen when you tried to warn me she had a different view of our friendship.'

He turned on Ellen, savagely sarcastic. 'So because you were jealous you kindly arranged for me to pursue my so-called ambitions unfettered, leaving Natalie to face her pregnancy alone. It didn't occur to you that it was *my* child too, that I might have preferred some say in how he was brought up? That I might have *wanted* to change my plans in order to be able to do so? What *right* did you have to take so much upon yourself?'

Ellen was almost whimpering under the lash of his anger. 'I'm sorry...I'm sorry... I know I shouldn't have meddled...and it didn't do any good anyway, because you stayed in America.'

'And thank the lord I did!' Daniel snarled. 'If you'd had your way Natalie and I would never have seen each other again. As it is, at least we've a chance of building something out of the mess your malice made. Oh, get out of my sight! Go and ring for a taxi to take you to the station. And wait for it outside,' he threw after her as she scurried away.

The receding click of Ellen's heels on the parquet left a heavy silence behind. Daniel finally broke it with a harsh, 'Well? For God's sake *say* something!'

Natalie eyed him warily. It was obvious there was still a lot of anger in him and, balked of his legitimate target, he seemed to be directing it at her. 'I'm still too punch-drunk to know what to say.'

He came to stand in front of her. 'Natalie, do you at least believe I did *not* desert you and Tim?'

'Oh, yes! How could I not believe it now?' She felt as if something oppressive had been lifted from her spirit and her eyes glowed. 'What is most incredible is not so much what Ellen did, destroying your letter and telling me you'd thrown me over for her, but the way everything conspired to play into her hands: your leaving some of your belongings with her, my having to leave Priorscombe before any of your further letters could reach me.'

Something struck her, something that should have made more of an impression before. 'Ellen said she took your letter when she was helping you pack for your trip to America. That couldn't be right, though. Surely you went to America much later?'

He shook his head. 'Right after I'd made that brief visit down here to see you, I realised that becoming a barrister was not quite the holy grail I'd thought it. I began to like the idea of us as a family, you, me and a baby, even if you weren't actually pregnant then. So I contacted Gilmorton, said I'd like to take up his offer, if it was still open. I nearly refused when he wanted to send me to America to bone up on US law, but then I thought if I could succeed anywhere it would be there. So I wrote and told you about it, told you I'd be back to marry you once I'd found a home for us.'

'Oh, Daniel,' she choked, 'you gave up your hopes of being a barrister for *me*? You planned all this before you knew it was even necessary?'

His fingers feathered against her lips, stopping her words. 'It was always necessary to me, Natalie.' His hands moved, framing her face, twining in the pale, silky hair. 'Right from the very first time I saw you, you became necessary to me. Nobody had ever caught at my heart-strings like you did. Something about you seemed to fill up all the empty spaces inside me.'

Natalie closed her eyes. She hadn't been wrong about him all those years ago. What he was saying echoed all her own feelings.

'I was so certain we were meant to be together,' he went on, 'that I didn't worry too much when I didn't get an immediate answer to my letter. I thought you were waiting to be really sure whether you were pregnant or not. I wrote again, because I thought you might need some reassurance, and still there was no reply. And then I heard you'd married someone else. Not just someone else but the man who was responsible for sending me out of the country, an old man, but very rich.' His arms tightened around her convulsively. 'God, Natalie, I felt as if I'd been crucified!'

Tears spiked Natalie's long eyelashes as she wound her arms around his waist, offering her silent sympathy and understanding, for she too had suffered the same anguish. 'In the light of Ellen's revelations, I can't blame you for believing there was some sort of conspiracy, that I was cynically marrying Hector for his money,' she said. 'How you must have hated me!'

'In equal proportion to how I'd loved you,' he confirmed morosely. 'And yet in a way it was probably good for me. I buried myself in my work. For one thing it helped to blunt the pain, and for another I was determined to show you, one day, just what you'd turned down.' He gave a low groan. 'And I did, didn't I? Throwing my weight about terrorising you, threatening, blackmailing. I couldn't believe it when I was sent a copy of Gilmorton's will. That he'd left *me* in charge! It seemed a heaven-sent opportunity to make you pay for what you'd done.'

He looked down gravely into her upturned face. 'I really did intend to take my son from you, you know. But then each time I saw you I didn't know whether I wanted to beat you or make love to you until you begged for mercy, until in the end I knew I had to have you too.'

His eyes seemed to burn her up, and Natalie's slight body trembled with the passion of her response. 'But what made you suspect Ellen? You were so adamant that I was lying when I tried to tell you my side of what had happened.'

'Oh, little things, but they built up into a different picture from the one I'd always imagined. The fact that you'd been a real mother to Gilmorton's daughter all these years instead of packing her off to boarding-school. Your sister-in-law scolding you for insisting on your husband willing you only a modest income. Your apparent contentment with a way of life that included little in the way of entertainment and certainly no extravagance, and what should have clinched it at once if I hadn't been so pigheaded: the fact that you *knew* I'd left books and clothes at Ellen's flat. And then last night...'

He shook his head, remembering. 'I know I hadn't gone the right way about persuading you to marry me—all that nonsense about only wanting you to get my son—but it really hurt when you said you wouldn't marry me because you couldn't trust me. By then I thought it would be little use to tell you I was beginning to suspect Ellen of having a hand in our split. If you weren't to go on believing I was the most untrustworthy bastard out you had to hear it all from Ellen herself.'

'I won't ask the methods you used to get her to confess...' Natalie smiled wryly '...having been on the receiving end of some of them myself.'

'Don't! Please don't remind me what an arrant fool I've been.' His arms tightened round her and they clung together, each giving and taking comfort for the pain of the years apart. 'You do trust me now, Natalie?'

He was so solid, the strong arms holding her so safe. 'Oh, yes,' she breathed, knowing she had come home.

'And you will marry me?' It was a new experience to hear the uncertain pleading in his voice.

She looked up at him, her face solemn, her trust so complete that she could say, half teasing, 'I did have *two* criteria before I married again; I had to be able to trust the man, and he had to love me.'

'I fell in love with an enchanting teenager...' his eyes roamed over her face, loving every detail '...and the silver threads of that enchantment hold me still, and will do for the rest of my life.'

The same threads that had such a tenacious hold on her own heart. Natalie smiled radiantly. 'I suppose we'll have to wait until Ginevra's finished her exams, but a couple of weeks should give Kitty time to organise everything she'll feel necessary for a wedding.'

Daniel gave a great shout and spun her off her feet. 'Oh, Natalie... I *do* love you... Come on, let's go and ask our son if he'd like to be a page-boy at our wedding.'

He hustled her out of the house and into his car. 'And our daughter a bridesmaid,' Natalie said. Then, slanting him a laughing glance across the space between them, 'And you might tell me what

Summer Reading
At Its Best

In July, Harlequin and Silhouette bring readers the Big Summer Read Program. Heat up your summer with these four exciting new novels by top Harlequin and Silhouette authors.

SOMEWHERE IN TIME by Barbara Bretton
YESTERDAY COMES TOMORROW by Rebecca Flanders
A DAY IN APRIL by Mary Lynn Baxter
LOVE CHILD by Patricia Coughlin

From time travel to fame and fortune, this program offers something for everyone.

Available at your favorite retail outlet.

BSR

JAYNE ANN KRENTZ

Dreams
Parts One & Two

The warrior died at her feet, his blood running out of the cave entrance and mingling with the waterfall. With his last breath he cursed the woman—told her that her spirit would remain chained in the cave forever until a child was created and born there....

So goes the ancient legend of the Chained Lady and the curse that bound her throughout the ages—until destiny brought Diana Prentice and Colby Savager together under the influence of forces beyond their understanding. Suddenly they were both haunted by dreams that linked past and present, while their waking hours were filled with danger. Only when Colby, Diana's modern-day warrior, learned to love, could those dark forces be vanquished. Only then could Diana set the Chained Lady free....

Back by Popular Demand

Janet Dailey
Americana

Janet Dailey takes you on a romantic tour of America through fifty favorite Harlequin Presents novels, each one set in a different state, and researched by Janet and her husband, Bill.

A journey of a lifetime. The perfect collectable series!

August titles   **#37 OREGON**
To Tell the Truth

#38 PENNSYLVANIA
The Thawing of Mara

"GET AWAY FROM IT ALL" SWEEPSTAKES

HERE'S HOW THE SWEEPSTAKES WORKS

NO PURCHASE NECESSARY

To enter each drawing, complete the appropriate Official Entry Form or a 3" by 5" index card by hand-printing your name, address and phone number and the trip destination that the entry is being submitted for (i.e., Caneel Bay, Canyon Ranch or London and the English Countryside) and mailing it to: Get Away From It All Sweepstakes, P.O. Box 1397, Buffalo, New York 14269-1397.

No responsibility is assumed for lost, late or misdirected mail. Entries must be sent separately with first class postage affixed, and be received by: 4/15/92 for the Caneel Bay Vacation Drawing, 5/15/92 for the Canyon Ranch Vacation Drawing and 6/15/92 for the London and the English Countryside Vacation Drawing. Sweepstakes is open to residents of the U.S. (except Puerto Rico) and Canada, 21 years of age or older as of 5/31/92.

For complete rules send a self-addressed, stamped (WA residents need not affix return postage) envelope to: Get Away From It All Sweepstakes, P.O. Box 4892, Blair, NE 68009.

© 1992 HARLEQUIN ENTERPRISES LTD. SWP-RLS

- -

"GET AWAY FROM IT ALL" SWEEPSTAKES

HERE'S HOW THE SWEEPSTAKES WORKS

NO PURCHASE NECESSARY

To enter each drawing, complete the appropriate Official Entry Form or a 3" by 5" index card by hand-printing your name, address and phone number and the trip destination that the entry is being submitted for (i.e., Caneel Bay, Canyon Ranch or London and the English Countryside) and mailing it to: Get Away From It All Sweepstakes, P.O. Box 1397, Buffalo, New York 14269-1397.

No responsibility is assumed for lost, late or misdirected mail. Entries must be sent separately with first class postage affixed, and be received by: 4/15/92 for the Caneel Bay Vacation Drawing, 5/15/92 for the Canyon Ranch Vacation Drawing and 6/15/92 for the London and the English Countryside Vacation Drawing. Sweepstakes is open to residents of the U.S. (except Puerto Rico) and Canada, 21 years of age or older as of 5/31/92.

For complete rules send a self-addressed, stamped (WA residents need not affix return postage) envelope to: Get Away From It All Sweepstakes, P.O. Box 4892, Blair, NE 68009.

© 1992 HARLEQUIN ENTERPRISES LTD. SWP-RLS

"GET AWAY FROM IT ALL"

Brand-new Subscribers-Only Sweepstakes

OFFICIAL ENTRY FORM

This entry must be received by: June 15, 1992
This month's winner will be notified by: June 30, 1992
Trip must be taken between: July 31, 1992—July 31, 1993

YES, I want to win the vacation for two to England. I understand the prize includes round-trip airfare and the two additional prizes revealed in the BONUS PRIZES insert.

Name _____

Address _____

City _____

State/Prov._____ Zip/Postal Code _____

Daytime phone number _____
                                          (Area Code)

Return entries with invoice in envelope provided. Each book in this shipment has two entry coupons — and the more coupons you enter, the better your chances of winning!
© 1992 HARLEQUIN ENTERPRISES LTD.   3M-CPN

"GET AWAY FROM IT ALL"

Brand-new Subscribers-Only Sweepstakes

OFFICIAL ENTRY FORM

This entry must be received by: June 15, 1992
This month's winner will be notified by: June 30, 1992
Trip must be taken between: July 31, 1992—July 31, 1993

YES, I want to win the vacation for two to England. I understand the prize includes round-trip airfare and the two additional prizes revealed in the BONUS PRIZES insert.

Name _____

Address _____

City _____

State/Prov._____ Zip/Postal Code _____

Daytime phone number _____
                                          (Area Code)

Return entries with invoice in envelope provided. Each book in this shipment has two entry coupons — and the more coupons you enter, the better your chances of winning!
© 1992 HARLEQUIN ENTERPRISES LTD.   3M-CPN